Hodder M. Westropp

Primitive Symbolism

as illustrated in phallic worship or the reproductive principle

Hodder M. Westropp

Primitive Symbolism
as illustrated in phallic worship or the reproductive principle

ISBN/EAN: 9783337291754

Printed in Europe, USA, Canada, Australia, Japan

Cover: Foto ©Andreas Hilbeck / pixelio.de

More available books at **www.hansebooks.com**

Two Volumes, Demy 4to, 1,270 pages, with Maps, numerous Illustrations, and large separate Chart. Price Six Guineas.

Rivers of Life;

OR,

SOURCES AND STREAMS OF THE FAITHS OF MAN IN ALL LANDS,

SHOWING THE

EVOLUTION OF FAITHS

FROM THE RUDEST SYMBOLISMS TO THE LATEST SPIRITUAL DEVELOPMENTS.

BY

MAJOR-GENERAL J. G. R. FORLONG,

F.R.G.S., F.R.S.E., M.A.I., A.I.C.E.,
F.R.H.S., F.R.A.Socy., &c., &c.

Contents of Vol. I.

Contents of Vol. II.

Appendixes.

I. A Coloured Chart of all Faith Streams, 7½ feet by 2¼ feet, either Folded or on Roller.

II. Map of World, as known about Second Century B.C., showing Early Races and Faiths.

III. Sketch Map of Ancient India, and from Baluchistan to Anam, showing Early Tribes, their Sacred Places, &c.

IV. Synoptical Table of Gods, God-Ideas, and many Features which all Faiths have more or less in Common. If on Roller this is 3 feet by 21 inches.

[P.T.O.

GENERAL FORLONG'S "RIVERS OF LIFE."

GENERAL FORLONG has now given to the public, in two magnificent quarto volumes and chart, the first instalment of his great work on comparative religion, and on the natural evolution of existing faiths, which has been in preparation for the last seven years.

The importance of this work consists in its being the first to apply the result of modern research and learning to the great subject of Asiatic religions in a thoroughly unbiased manner. No one can read the long list of General Forlong's authorities without seeing that he is well up to date in his reading, although he has also consulted many valuable authorities now rarely read, being contained in ponderous and expensive folios. The works of Max Müller, Rhys Davies, Beal, Cox, Sayce, and many other standard authorities on oriental subjects; of Birch and Brugsch, Renouf and Maspero in Egypt, of Haug West and Darmesteter in Persia, together with the latest accounts of travellers in Palestine, in China, in Africa, and America, have all been ransacked for information. General Forlong is generally able to show how little many writers really know of the meaning of the customs, traditions, symbolisms, and superstitions concerning which they write.

The volumes are accompanied by a large separate Chart (price £2), which will be found very useful for students anxious to obtain a clear idea of the relation and antiquity of the different religious systems, and of the constituents of those systems. The various cults of the Tree, the Serpent and Lingam, the Fire, the Ancestor, and the Sun, with the later more spiritual conceptions of deity as a Father and a Spirit, are distinguished by coloured streams; and the student at a glance can see which of these ideas is embraced by any existing creed.

Many valuable data, chronological and physical, mythological and ethnical, are given on the margin of the chart, and all the great Bibles of Asia, and Africa, and Europe, are shown in relative position.

General Forlong's chief claim to speak on these questions lies in the fact that he is not a mere bookworm or compiler but an active explorer, and a student who has visited the sacred places of which he treats, and has received from the lips of living Brahmans and Bikshus their own interpretation of the symbolism of the ancient Faiths of India. When General Forlong wished to understand Rome or Delphi, Jerusalem or Shechem, he visited those places himself, just as he has visited the famous Indian sites, and as in our own islands, he has studied the ruder stone monuments of England, Scotland, and Ireland on the spot, and by the light of existing remains in India and else-where. In cases where he has not so visited the site, he has diligently collected the most recent and authentic information, and with such knowledge of his subjects he combines, as we have seen, a wide reading of the latest and the earliest literature regarding them in some 700 books, many in eight or ten volumes each. The illustrations alone of his work, many of which are admirably bold sketches from the original, are of the greatest value to the student, and his volumes, with their careful indexes, form a storehouse of research and learning, in which future writers might dig long without exhausting material.

Copies may be obtained from the Publisher of the present volume.

PRIMITIVE SYMBOLISM,

AS ILLUSTRATED IN

PHALLIC WORSHIP.

PRIMITIVE SYMBOLISM

AS ILLUSTRATED IN

𝔓𝔥𝔞𝔩𝔩𝔦𝔠 𝔚𝔬𝔯𝔰𝔥𝔦𝔭

OR

THE REPRODUCTIVE PRINCIPLE

BY

HODDER M. WESTROPP

WITH AN INTRODUCTION BY

GENERAL FORLONG

F.R.G.S., F.R.S.E., M.A.I., A.I.C.E., F.R.H.S., F.R.A.S., ETC.,
AUTHOR OF "RIVERS OF LIFE."

LONDON

GEORGE REDWAY

YORK STREET COVENT GARDEN

M DCCC LXXXV.

INTRODUCTION.

This work is a *multum in parvo* of the growth and spread of Phallicism, as we commonly call the worship of nature or fertilizing powers. I felt, when solicited to enlarge and illustrate it on the sudden death of the lamented author, that it would be desecration to touch so complete a compendium by one of the most competent and soundest thinkers who have written on this world-wide faith. None knew better or saw more clearly than Mr. Westropp that in this oldest symbolism and worship lay the foundations of all the goodly systems we call Religions; but unfortunately, though writing clearly, he has only left to us short and somewhat detached Essays, this being the longest I have come across. It was, therefore, with deep concern I heard of his death, and saw his perhaps last note pencilled at the end of the proof-sheets—" Confined to bed with a severe attack of dyspepsia."

He read a Paper, which justly attracted much attention, in 1870, before the Anthropological Society, London, in the days when such subjects were then possible, as they are not now, owing to admission of lady members. Mr. J. W. Bouton, of New York, incorporated this in 1875 with Mr. Staniland Wake's valuable Paper of the same period and some others, the whole forming his useful publication entitled *Ancient Symbol Worship in the Religions of Antiquity*. Many of the facts there stated—as true for all time and necessary to show the continuity of the

faith—will be found in the present epitome, our only
regret being that this short historical summary does not
extend further in time and space as down to these days
and islands, indeed to Europe in general, for Mr.
Westropp's researches had assured him that if the old
worships are now only dimly perceptible it is not yet so
with the ancient symbolisms—nay, the tendency has been
to amplify these, especially in ecclesiastical architecture,
ornamentation, rites, vestments, &c. He appears to have
been, from divers causes, averse to drive facts and arguments home into the midst of existing faiths and sacred
books, for this is to increase the dislike naturally inherent
to the subject, and to wound many of the tenderest emo-
tions of a large class, especially of the more ignorant
adherents of our own and other Religions. These cannot
distinguish between the religious student of ancient and
modern art, tracing the various growths of cults in symbols
and rituals, from the sceptic or worse, who has come to
pull down the sacred groves and gods, and thus uproot
all the cherished feelings with which their holy objects,
rites and festivals inspire them. They are willing to smile
over the idea of the origin of a church spire or temple
minaret, and to laugh at what they think is the mere
ingenuity of the inquirer, but they frown when the inquiry
goes further, and solid facts are advanced proving that their
faith is in every detail a mere evolution of Faiths that
preceded it, just as they themselves are of previous men.
They are willing to accept from a poetical point of view
that " there has been no entirely new religion from the
beginning of the world," and from a philological, that
our alphabet has evolved from previous alphabets, and
these from some scratchings of savage tribes, but not to

carry such evolution theories beyond or into their fancied divine ideals. Yet if we are to instruct people aright or to investigate an important subject we must do so thoroughly, and, marshalling our facts, show their far-reaching significance in all their bearings, at least so far as the instructed are capable of comprehending, and not to that extent only which they may prefer. The ancient priest had his esoteric and exoteric doctrines and mysteries, with the object of alluring and keeping within his fold all manner of men, women and children, but here we speak unto men *caring only that they know the truth,* not that they be won over to our view or that of any other, but that they act according to their lights. Mr. Westropp here takes the best course in the present crass ignorance of Europe by simply massing together a few pregnant facts. He avoids the doubtful and all that may lead to controversy and annoyance, and calmly rehearses his case as a philosopher, physician and friend, who desires that the inquirer should know something of his "whence and whither," at least so far as the study of history and humanity can teach him. We must here say a few words regarding the author's very apposite quotations on p. 41, for they point to the radical difference between real *religion* and *"Religions."*

These have been always more or less superstitions or beliefs resting mainly on priestly assertions, unproved and often incomprehensible, regarding supernatural Powers, deities, or spirits and events in the *quasi* histories of these, according to, and on account of which, the followers of these ideals were required to shape their conduct, nay, their very thoughts. This was the original idea of *a* Religion, but such is *no true religion,* for this simply consists of living a just, moral and righteous life, guided by the highest ethical ideas we have each attained unto. The _Religens_ or "Religious ones" were simply those who separated themselves from what they called "the world" in order to serve their gods, banding themselves together in solitary places, caves, temples, monasteries, &c., so as the better to observe (_Réligio_) their vows, rites and laws. These last they believed came from their _Theos_, Allah or other divine Rex, Regis or Prophet. All tribes had laws given to them by their priests, of which, perhaps, the most perfect specimen is the _Dharma_ and _Vināya_, the _themis_—"Heavenly Law and Way or Discipline" of Budhists. The original meaning of _Relegare_—"to bind fast"—was simply a consecration to one particular purpose, not necessarily a holy one. The priests relegated themselves, we may say, to continually reading over, reviewing, or going back upon the services of their gods—for ever rehearsing praises and prayers to them in order to please them and avert calamities which they feared. It was no part of the design of the _Religens_ to serve or please their fellows, to inculcate virtue, honour, truth, goodness, or even chastity, not to speak of a high moral and intellectual life. The truly "Religious" or "Holy man" was, as such, entirely _un_moral. He did not admit that the ethics which guided him in his social or family life had any place within the hallowed circle of his temple or faith. Here he knew of no morality or immorality; all symbols, rites and customs of the faith were divine, and, as regards the sanctuary, he was but the servant of his god, striving _only to honour and serve Him,_ and for this purpose seeking even to debase himself by the most shocking and heinous offences, such as he would not, if otherwise a good man, for a moment tolerate in the family circle. Thus there was neither shame nor immorality in the rites of Militta described by Hêrodotos, nor in the priestly functions practised to this day by the Gosains or "Māha Rājas" of Krishna; nor in the Jewish leader giving a share of the captured Midian women "to the Lord" (Num. xxxi. 40); nor yet in "the Lord's house" being full of shameless women, and worse. *Religions* were not practical guides for the world, but for the *Religens* and the services of the sanctuary, and only practical and pious philosophers like Confucius and Budha strove to supply to mankind *real religion.* Even Paul taught that "the wisdom of the Greeks"—morals or "works," and intellectual attainments, "were foolishness"—worldly matters beneath the notice of the truly "religious;" that the ignorant faith of a babe was what men should strive for, and following Paul, all the Christian fathers with few exceptions, down to even Luther and Calvin, taught very similar doctrine. "Religion," they said, was a Faith, *pistis*, "belief" or "loyalty" to the god-idea and tales concerning the god or his incarnations, and the greatest sin or "irreligion" was *āpistia*, or want of faith. So Mahamadans call their "Religion" *Islām*, or "Faith," and only Islāmis are accepted by Allah. Luther was horrified at much of the writing of *James.* He called it "an epistle of sham and by no apostle," because that writer asks with amazement, "Can faith save any one?" Jerome frequently urges that all secular improvement only merits divine punishment, and virtually that those who ignore all physical, social and moral laws "are children of the unseen but heavenly kingdom." No good Christian doubted that unbelievers were to be damned (though our beliefs can only follow the laws of evidence), and that men like Galileo, Bruno, &c., however moral, good and pious in the best sense of these words, were justly condemned to fire here and hereafter. On these grounds also, Greeks murdered Sōkrātes, well known for piety, justice, and righteousness, and banished unbelieving Aristotle, Protagoras, and others from their highly " Religious" society. St. Augustine was in the habit of saying of such really religious men : *predestinati sunt in æternum ignem ire cum diabolo ;* and many Christians besides Ignatius Loyola urged that " the highest virtue in a Christian is the sacrifice of the intellect," and the greatest sin, " listening to the dictates of reason."

In all this we see the childhood of true *religion*, which is now sapping the foundations of what is called " *Religions*." Mr. Westropp shows their fundamental phase, or that substratum from which a beautiful plant is now vigorously putting forth its strength in a few favoured localities ; for *Nature worship* is still the prevalent " Religion" of the world, and Her Majesty rules over six Worshippers of the Reproductive Powers for every Christian in her vast empire. It behoves us, therefore, to study these matters if we would know what so-called *Religions* really are.

J. G. R. FORLONG.

PHALLIC WORSHIP.

THE identity of human nature and of the human mind, in all times and in all countries, is the key to the solution of many phenomena in the development of man's mind and nature.

Human nature is one and the same everywhere. The same wants beget the invention and use of the same means to supply those wants.

The workings of man's mind, being obedient to similar laws, are the same, and the thoughts, suggestions, ideas and actions proceeding from them, nearly identical in all countries ; the same ideas arise within the mind of man, suggested by the same objects.

Hence similar and analogous ideas, beliefs, and superstitious practices are frequently evolved independently among different peoples. These are the result of suggestions arising spontaneously in the human mind at certain stages of its development, and which seem almost universal.

As a remarkable instance of this, I have drawn up the following sketch of phallic worship, which is one of those beliefs or superstitious practices which have sprung up independently and spontaneously, and which seems to have extensively prevailed among many nations.

It will acquire additional interest when it is considered that it is one of, if not the most ancient of the supersti-

tions of the human race,* that it has prevailed more or
less among all known peoples in ancient times, and that it
has been handed down even to a very late and Christian
period.

In the earlier ages the operations of nature made a
stronger impression on the minds of men. Those ideas,
springing from the constant observation of the modes of
acting in nature, were consequently more readily suggested
to the minds of all races of men in the primitive ages.

Two causes must have forcibly struck the minds of
men in those early periods when observant of the operations of nature, one the generative power, the other the
re-productive, the active and the passive causes. This
two-fold mode of production visible in nature must have
given rise to comparisons with the mode of proceeding in
the generation of animals, in which two causes concur,
the one active and the other passive; the one male and
the other female, the one as father, the other as mother.
These ideas were doubtless suggested independently
and spontaneously in different countries; for the human
mind is so constituted that the same objects and the same
operations of nature will suggest like ideas in the minds
of men of all races, however widely apart.

Nature to the early man was not brute matter, but a
being invested with his own personality, and endowed
with the same feelings, passions, and performing the same
functions. He could only conceive the course of nature
from the analogy to his own actions. By "an easy illu-

---

* Sex worship is as ancient as star worship, if not more so. Such
phallicism was the exponent of the principle of renewal and reproduction. It was the most natural form of expressing the idea of creation.
—*Bonwick, Egyptian Belief, p.* 258.

sion " the functions of human nature were transferred to physical nature. Man not only attributed his own mind and feelings to the powers of nature, but also the functions of his nature—generation, begetting—re-production, bringing forth; they became his ideas of cause and effect. To the Sun the great fecundator, and the chief cause of awakening nature into life; to the Earth, the great recipient, in the bosom of which all things are produced, man attributed the same powers and modes of re-production as in human nature. The human intellect being finite, man is incapable of imagining a personal god inseparable from the functions of human nature. Sex was given to them; the Sun or sky was considered the male, or active power; the Earth, the female or passive power. The sky was the fecundating and fertilizing power; the earth was looked upon as the mould of nature, as the recipient of seeds, the nurse of what was produced in its bosom. An analogy was suggested in the union of the male and female. These comparisons are found in ancient writers. " The bright sky," Æschylus* says, " loves to penetrate the earth ; the earth, on her part, aspires to the heavenly marriage. Rain falling from the watery sky impregnates the earth, and she produces for mortals pastures of the flocks, and the gifts of Ceres." " The sky," Plutarch says, " appeared to men to perform the functions of a father, as the earth those of a mother. The sky was the father, for it cast seed into the bosom of the earth, which on receiving them became fruitful and brought forth, and was the mother." This union has been sung in the following verses by Virgil :—†

---

* *Danaides (Frag.* 45, *Herm.*)   † *Georg.* ii. 325.

Tum pater omnipotens fecundis imbribus Æther
Conjugis in gremium lætæ descendit.

Columella has related, in his treatise on agriculture, the loves of nature, or the marriage of heaven and earth, which takes place at the spring of the year.

" Reverence for the mystery of organized life," as Mrs. Child writes, " led to the recognition of a masculine and feminine principle in all things spiritual or material. Every elemental force was divided into two, the parents of other forces. The active mind was masculine, the productive earth was feminine."

" Eminent scholars," remarks Dr. Ginsburg (*Moabite Stone*, page 43), " who have devoted themselves to the investigation of ancient cults, have shown to demonstration that the most primitive idea of God was that he consisted of a dual nature, masculine and feminine, and the connubial contact of this androgynous Deity gave birth to creation."

" The divine power in creation," as Mr. Bonwick writes, " was always regarded among the ancients from a generative point of view." *

These ideas bear a prominent part in the religious creeds of several nations. In Egypt the Deity or principle of generation was Khem, called " the father "—the abstract idea of father, as the goddess Maut was that of mother. The office of Khem was not confined to the

---

* The first verse of the Book of Genesis declares creation to have been a series of *Toledoth*, or generations. It is properly translated " God (the Elohim—or rather *Alé-im*) engendered (B'RA) the heavens and the earth." In the language of Plato :—" The Supreme God generated the gradual succession of dependant spirits, of gods, of dæmons, of heroes and of men.

procreation and continuation of the human species, but extended even to the vegetable world, over which he presided, when we find his statue accompanied by trees and plants; and kings offering to him herbs of the ground, cutting the corn before him, or employed in his presence tilling the land, and preparing it to receive the generating influence of the deity. Khem was styled *Ammon generator,* and was represented *ithyphallic.*

As Mr. Bonwick writes, "When Ammon, Ptah, Khem, Osiris, or Horus appear in ithyphallic guise, it is in their condition as the Demiurgus, by whom the worlds were made."

At Philæ Osiris was worshipped as the generating cause, and Isis the receptive mould.

At Mendis Osiris was considered to be the male principle, and Isis a form of the female principle. Plutarch tells us in his *Isis and Osiris* that in the Egyptian belief, when a planet entered into a sign, their conjunction was denominated a marriage.

Synesius gives an inscription on an Egyptian deity, "Thou art the father and thou art the mother. Thou art the male and thou art the female."

Mr. Mahaffy, in his *Prolegomena,* p. 267, gives the following Egyptian text :—"God is the sun himself incarnate; his commencement is from the beginning. He is the God who has existed of old. There is no God without him. A mother hath not borne him, nor a father begotten him. GOD-GODDESS created from himself, all the gods have existed as soon as he began." Upon the latter phrases Mr. Chabas remarks, "These two latter phrases are the most exact formula, the most simple of Egyptian theology, such as it was taught in the highest system of initiation. A sole deity, invested with the power of production—that is to say, *of the two principles, male and female*—he created himself before all things, and the arrival of the gods was only a diffusion, a manifestation of his different faculties and of his all-powerful will." In a hymn the deity is thus addressed, "Glory to thee who hast begotten all that exists, who hast made man, who hast made the gods."

The Egyptian Triads were composed of father, mother, and son—that is, the male and female principles of nature, with their product.

In the *Saiva Purána* of the Hindus, Siva says: "From the supreme spirit proceed Purusha (the generative or male principle), Prakriti (the productive or female principle), and Time; and by them was produced this universe, the manifestation of one God. . . . Of all organs of sense and intellect, the best is mind, which proceeds from Ahankara, Ahankara from intellect, intellect from the supreme being, who is, in fact, Purusha. It is the primeval male, whose form constitutes the universe, and whose breath is the sky; and though incorporeal, that male am I."

In the Kritya Tatwa, Siva is thus addressed by Bráhma; "I know that Thou, O Lord, art the eternal Brahm, that seed which, being received in the womb of the Sakti (aptitude to conceive), produced this universe; that thou united with thy Sakti dost create the universe from this own substance like the web from the spider." In the same creed Siva is described as the personification of Surya, the sun; Agni, the fire, or genial heat which pervades, generates, and vivifies all; he is

Bhāva, the lord of Bhavānī the universal mother, goddess of nature and of the earth.

In one of the hymns of the Rig Veda quoted by Professor Monier Williams (*Hinduism*, p. 26) we perceive the first dim outline of the remarkable idea that the Creator willed to produce the universe through the agency and co-operation of a female principle—an idea which afterwards acquired more definite shape in the supposed marriage of heaven and earth. In the Veda also various deities were regarded as the progeny resulting from the fancied union of Earth with Dyaus, " heaven;" just as much of the later mythology may be explained by a supposed blending of the male and female principles in nature. In the *Sama-Veda* (viii. p. 44) the idea is more fully expressed : " He felt not delight, being alone. He wished another, and instantly became such. He caused his own self to fall in twain, and thus became husband and wife. He approached her, and thus were produced human beings."

"Brahma," the creator, writes Professor Williams, "was made to possess a double nature, or, in other words, two characters—one quiescent, the other active. The active was called his Sakti, and was personified as his wife, or the female half of his essence. The Sakti of the creator ought properly to represent the female creative capacity, but the idea of the blending of the male and female principles in creation seems to have been transferred to Siva and his Sakti Parvati. One of the representatives of Siva is half-male and half-female, emblematic of the indissoluble unity of the creative principle (hence his name, *Ard-hanâ risá*, the half female lord ").

Siva represented the Fructifying Principle, the generating power that pervades the universe, producing sun, moon, stars, men, animals, and plants. His wife, or Sakti, was Parvati, for each divine personage was associated with a consort, to show that male and female, man and wife, are ever indissolubly united as the sources of reproduction.

In China, according to Prof. Muller,* we find the recognition of two powers, one active, the other passive, one male, the other female, which comprehend everything, and which, in the mind of the more enlightened, tower high above the great crowd of minor spirits. These two powers are within and beneath and behind everything that is double in nature, and they have been frequently identified with heaven and earth. In the *Shu-King* we are told that heaven and earth together are the father and mother of all things.

At the head of the Babylonian mythology stands a deity who was sometimes identified with the heavens, sometimes considered as the ruler and god of heaven. This deity is named Anu. He represents the universe as the upper and lower regions, and when these were divided the upper region or heaven was called Anu, while the lower region or earth was called Anatu. Anu being the male principle, and Anatu the female principle, or wife of Anu.

The successive forms, Lahina and Lahama, Sar and Kisar, are represented in some of the god lists as names or manifestations of Anu and Anatu. In each case there appears to be a male and female principle, which principles combine in the formation of the universe.†

---

* Lectures on the Science of Religion.

† Smith's *Chaldæan Genesis*, p. 54.

Among the Assyrians the supreme god, Bel, was styled "the procreator;" and his wife, the goddess Mylitta, represented the productive principle of nature, and received the title of the queen of fertility. Among the Assyrian deities, writes Dr. Ginsburg (*Moabite stone*, page 43), "the name Ashtar or Ashter means generative power, tied together, joined, coupled connubial contact, whilst Astarte is the feminine half or companion of the productive power."

Another deity, the god Vul, the god of the atmosphere, is styled the beneficent chief, the giver of abundance, the lord of fecundity. On Assyrian cylinders he is represented as a phallic deity. With him is associated a goddess Shala, whose ordinary title is "Sarrat," queen, the feminine of the word "Sar," which means chief. Sir Henry Rawlinson remarks with regard to the Assyrian Sun, or Shamas, the sun-god, that the idea of the motive influence of the sun-god in all human affairs arose from the manifest agency of the material sun in stimulating the functions of Nature. On the Moabite stone the god of the Moabites is called Ashtar-Chemosh—Chemosh meaning *the conqueror*, and Ashtar *the producer*—a joint name, which implies an androgynous (male and female) deity. In Phœnician mythology, Ouranos (heaven) weds Ghè (the earth), and by her becomes father of Oceanus, Hyperion, Iapetus, Cronos, and other gods. In conformity with the religious ideas of the Greeks and Romans, Virgil describes the products of the earth as the result of the conjugal act between Jupiter (the sky) and Juno (the earth.) According to St. Augustin the sexual organ of man was consecrated in the temple of Liber, that of woman in the sanctuaries of Liberia; these two divinities were named father and mother. According to Payne Knight, Priapus, in his character of a procreative deity, is celebrated by the Greek poets under the title of Love or Attraction, the first principle of animation; the father of gods and men, and the regulator and dispenser of all things. He is said to pervade the universe with the motion of his wings, bringing pure light; and thence to be called "the splendid, the self illumined, the ruling Priapus." In Greece he was regarded as the promoter of fertility both in vegetation and in all animals. According to Natalis Comes, the worship of Priapus was introduced at Athens by virtue of a command of an oracle.

Among the paintings found at Pompeii there are several representations of sacrifices of goats, and offerings of milk and flowers to Priapus. The god is represented as a Hermes on a square pedestal, with the usual characteristics of the deity, a prominent phallus. Similar Hermæ or Priapi were placed at the meeting of two or three roads. One of these paintings represents a sacrifice or offering to Priapus, made by two persons. The first is a young man with a dark skin, entirely naked, except the animal's skin, which is wrapt round his loins; his head is encircled with a wreath of leaves. He carries in his hands a basket in which are flowers and vegetables, the first offerings of his humble farm. He bends to place them at the foot of a small altar on which is a small statue in bronze representing the god of gardens. On the other side is a woman, also wearing a wreath, and dressed in a yellow tunic with green drapery. She holds in her left hand a golden dish, and in her right a vase. She appears to be bringing to the god of gardens an offering of milk:—

" Sinum lactis, et hæc te liba, Priape, quotannis
Expectare sat est : custos es pauperis horti."

Virgil, Ecl. vii., 33.

Offerings were made to Priapus according to the season
of the year :—

"Vere rosa, autumno pomis, æstate frequentor
Spicis: una mihi est horrida pestis hyems."

Priap. Veter, Epigr. 96.

In another painting Priapus is represented as placed on
a square stone, against which rest two sticks. The statue
appears to be of bronze. Its head is covered with a cap,
he has a small mantle on his shoulder, and exhibits his
usual prominent characteristic. The statue is evidently
placed by the road side, and he holds a stick in his hand
to point out the way to travellers. In a Priapic figure of
bronze he is styled Σωτὴρ Κόσμου as his symbol contributed
to the reproduction and perpetuation of mankind. Mutinus
was among the Romans the same as Priapus among the
Greeks, as they both were personifications of the fructifying
power of Nature. According to Herodotus and Pau-
sanias statues of Mercury were represented as ithyphallic.
The latter mentions one in particular at Cyllene.

In Mr. F. V. Dickens' "A Brief Account of the chief
cosmical ideas now current among the better educated
classes in Japan" he writes:—"In the Japanese creed
there are two elemental principles from the combination
of which everything originates—a Male, or developing one,
and a Female, or receptive one. The Earth is supposed
to have been formed by the condensation of the Female
principle in the middle of the Heavens; the Sun, on the
contrary, was the product of the great Male principle."

In the Sintoo creed in Japan, Heaven, or the sky,

married the Earth and became the author of mankind, having first raised up the dry land for their abode, beginning with the island of Kiu-Siu, by fishing it up with his spear from the bottom of the ocean.

We find similar ideas in the religious creeds of America and of the remote islands of the Pacific Ocean. According to the Indians of Central America, Famagostad and Zipaltonal, the first male and the second female, created heaven and earth, man and all things.

"As in Oriental legends," writes Mr. Brinton,* "the origin of man from the earth was veiled under the story that he was the progeny of some mountain fecundated by the embrace of Mithras or Jupiter, so the Indians often pointed to some height or some cavern, as the spot whence the first of men issued, adult and armed from the womb of the all-mother Earth.

The Tahitians imagined that everything which exists in the universe proceeds from the union of two beings; one of them was named Taroataihetounou; the other Tepapa; they were supposed to produce continually and by connection the days and months. These islanders supposed that the sun and moon, which are gods, had begotten the stars, and that the eclipses were the time of their copulation.

A New Zealand myth says we have two primeval ancestors, a father and a mother. They are Rangi and Papa, heaven and earth. The earth, out of which all things are produced, is our mother; the protecting and over-ruling heaven is our father.

It is thus evident that the doctrine of the reciprocal principles of nature, or nature active and passive, male

* *Myths of the Old World,* p. 224.

and female, was recognised in nearly all the primitive religious systems of the old as well as of the new world, and none more clearly than in those of Central America; thus proving not only the wide extent of the doctrine, but also a separate and independent origin, springing from those innate principles which are common to human nature in all climes and races. Hence the almost universal reverence paid to the images of the sexual parts, as they were regarded as symbols and types of the generative and productive principles in nature, and of those gods and goddesses who were the representatives of the same principles. " The first doctrine to be taught men would have relation to their being. The existence of a creator could be illustrated by a potter at the wheel. But there was a much more expressive form familiar to them, indicative of cause and effect in the production of births in the tribe, or in nature. In this way the *phallus* became the exponent of creative power ; and, though to our eyes vulgar and indecent, bore no improper meaning to the simple ancient worshipper."—Bonwick, *Egyptian Belief*, p. 257. The Phallus and the Kteis, the Lingam and the Yoni—the special parts contributing to generation and production—becoming thus symbols of those active and passive causes, could not fail to become objects of reverence and worship. The union of the two symbolized the creative energy of all nature ; for almost all primitive religion consisted in the reverence and worship paid to nature and its operations.

We may remark further, that the custom of worshipping what contributes to our wants and necessities, is frequently met with among uncivilised races. "In India," says Dubois, " a woman adores the basket which serves to bring or to hold necessaries, and offers sacrifices to it, as well as to the rice mill, and other implements that assist her in her household labours. A carpenter does the like homage to his hatchet, his adze, and other tools, and likewise offers sacrifice to them. A Brahman does so to the style with which he is going to write; a soldier to the arms he is to use in the field; a mason to his trowel; and a labourer to his plough." Hence it becomes intelligible that the organs of generation, which contribute to the production of living things, should receive worship and reverence.

Evidence that this worship of the organs of generation extensively prevailed will be found in many countries, both in ancient and modern times. It occurs in ancient Egypt, in India, in Syria, in Babylon, in Persia, Greece, Italy, Spain, Germany, Scandinavia, among the Gauls, and even in America among the Mexicans and Peruvians. In Egypt the phallus is frequently represented as the symbol of generation. Numerous writers have maintaiued that the *ankh,* or T, *(tau)* as the sign of life, was the phallus; and the *crux ansata* ♀ the combined male and female organs : just as the *sistrum,* or guitar of Egypt, and the *delta* Δ (lands on which the gods played and produced all life) represented Isis or "woman."*

Herodotus thus describes a festival in Egypt, which he had evidently seen himself:—"The festival is celebrated almost

---

* In the Egyptian hieroglyphics homonyms are frequently used, that is, words with two meanings, one that of an idea, the other that of an object. In the hieroglyphs, the object was put for the idea—thus *neter* means both "God" and "hatchet;" so a hatchet was placed for "God; again *nofre* means "good" and a "guitar;" the guitar therefore was placed for "good."

exactly as Bacchic festivals in Greece. They also use instead of phalli another invention consisting of images a cubit high, pulled by strings, which the women carry round to the villages. The virile member of these figures is scarcely less than the rest of the body, and this member they contrive to move. A piper goes in front and the women follow, singing hymns in honour of Bacchus." These figures doubtless represented the god Khem or the generative principle.

Among the royal offerings to Amen by Rameses III. in the Great Harris Papyrus are loaves (called Taenhannu) in the form of the phallus.

In the Pamelia the Egyptians exhibited a statue provided with three phalli. In the festivals of Bacchus, who was considered the same as Osiris, celebrated by Ptolemy Philadelphus, a gilt phallus, 120 cubits high, was carried in procession.

The phallus, so conspicuous in Egyptian theology, was associated with another idea than creation. It expressed resurrection. For this reason, it was pictured on coffins, and in tombs it told survivors that there was hope in the future. Vitality was not extinct. Upon this Mariette finely observes, " These images only symbolize in a very impressive manner the creative force of nature, without obscene intention. It is another way to express *celestial generation,* which should cause the deceased to enter a new life."

Ithyphallic representations set forth the resurrection of the body. In Denon's *Egypte* is figured the representation of a god with a green face, a sun's disk on each side, and stars around, while below the prominent member sat several small figures, as men waiting for the exertion of the resurrecting power of the deity.

The Viscount de Rougé gives the following description
of a scene represented on a sarcophagus :—" The right
side presents six personages in the attitude of prayer before a body without head, shut up in an egg.   This ithyphallic body's seed is collected by the first two personages.
This scene symbolizes the perpetual cycle of life, which is
re-born from the dead."

According to Ptolemy, the phallus was the object of
religious worship among the Abyssinians, and also among
the Persians.   In Syria Baal-Peor was represented with
a phallus in his mouth, according to St. Jerome.   At the
entrance of the temple at Hieropolis, a human figure,
with a phallus of monstrous size, of 120 cubits in height,
was to be observed.   Twice each year a man mounted to
the top of this colossus, by the means of a cord and a
piece of wood, fixed in the phallus, and on.which he
placed his foot.   This man passed, it is said, seven days
and seven nights on this phallus, without sleeping.   It
was thought that thus raised above the earth and nearer
the abode of the gods, this man could offer up vows
with more success, and thus many claimed the assistance
of his prayers, by placing precious gifts at the foot of the
phallus.   The Jews did not escape this worship, and we
see their women manufacturing phalli of gold and of
silver, as we find in Ezekiel xvi. 17.   General Forlong
(*Rivers of Life*, I. 158—170) advances arguments showing that the god of the Jewish ark was a sexual symbol
called, as in Exodus (xvi. 34), the *eduth*.

Among the Hindoos a religious reverence was extensively paid to the Lingam and the Yoni.   From time
immemorial, a symbol (the linga and yoni combined) has
been worshipped in Hindostan as the type of creation, or

the origin of life. It is the most common symbol of Siva, and is universally connected with his worship.*

"In the character of the eternal reproductive powers of nature," writes Prof. Monier Williams, "he is rather represented by a symbol (the linga and yoni combined) than by any human personification, and temples to hold

* The following description of a linga made out of a single chryso-beryl is taken from *The Times* of Oct. 11th, 1882 :—A CHRYSOBERYL LINGA.—An emblem of a primitive cult, which in varied forms appears in the mythology of India, Greece, Egypt, and the Semitic peoples among others, and which in India has survived to the present day, has recently been placed for a time in the collection of Mr. Bryce Wright, the mineralogist. This curious jewelled symbol of the re-productive powers of nature, which to Anglo-Indians is known as the Hindoo Lingam god, is formed of a fine pear-shaped chrysoberyl, or cat's eye stone, representing the linga of the followers of Siva, set in a great yellow topaz as an altar, the *yoni* or image of fertility of the followers of Vishnu. A band of diamonds encircles the setting of the topaz, which is about 1⅜ of an inch in its greatest length, and below, round the stand of gold, in the form of a truncated cone, are placed in obvious symbolism large precious stones—a ruby, a sapphire, a pale yellow chrysoberyl, coral, a pearl, a hyacinthine, or deep amber-coloured garnet, a pale yellow sapphire, an emerald, and a diamond. The gold is of 22 carat fineness, and the height of the whole idol is 2⅝ inch. According to writers on precious stones, the cat's eye chrysoberyl is a gem held in esteem among the Hindoos next to the diamond, and it is regarded by the common people not only as a charm against witchcraft, but as conferring good luck on the possessor. This one is of dark brown, the mobile ray of opalescent light crossing the height of the stone in an oblique direction. Its history can be traced for some 1700 years, and an admirer of the gem has tried to compute the number of millions of Hindoo women who had journeyed from all India to pay their devotion to the god in the 1,000 years before it was seized by a Mahommedan conqueror. On the breaking out of the mutiny in 1857, it was removed by the Queen of Delhi, and she parted with it to the present owner."

In the collection of Dr. Wise is a lingam, of about 6 inches long, of that rare stone green aventurine, with the head of Siva carved on it.

this symbol, which is of a double form to express the blending of the male and female principles in creation, are probably the most numerous of any temples now to be seen in India." It is usually placed in the inmost recess or sanctuary, sculptured in granite, marble or ivory, often crowned with flowers, and surmounted by a golden star. Lamps are kept burning before it, and on festival occasions it is illuminated by a lamp with seven branches, supposed to represent the planets. Small images of this emblem, carved in ivory, gold, or crystal, are often worn as ornaments about the neck. The Taly which the Brahmin consecrates, which the newly-married man attaches to the neck of his wife, and which she was bound to wear as long as she lived, is usually a Lingam. The pious use them in their prayers, and often have them buried with them. Devotees of Siva have it written on their foreheads in the form of a perpendicular mark. Each follower of Siva is bound to perform the Abichegam, a ceremony which consists, according to Sonnerat, in pouring milk on the lingam.

These symbols are found in the temple excavations of the Islands of Salsette and Elephanta, of unknown antiquity; on the grotto-temples of Ellora, at the " Seven Pagodas," on the Corómandel coast, in the old temple at Tanjore, and elsewhere where Siva worship is in the ascendant.

The extent to which the Linga Worship prevails throughout India is thus noticed by Professor Wilson in the *Asiatic Researches*. " Its prevalence throughout the whole tract of the Ganges, as far as Benares, is sufficiently conspicuous. In Bengal, the temples are commonly erected in a range of six, eight, or twelve, on each side of a ghaut leading to the river. Each of the temples in Bengal consists of a single chamber, of a square form, surmounted by a pyramidal centre; the area of each is very small; the *Linga*, of black or white marble, occupies the centre; the offerings are presented at the threshold. Benares, however, is the peculiar seat of this form of worship, the principal deity, Visweswara, "The Lord of all," is a linga, and most of the chief objects of the pilgrimage are similar blocks of stone. Particular divisions of the pilgrimage direct visiting forty-seven *Lingas*, all of pre-eminent sanctity; but there are hundreds of inferior note still worshipped, and thousands whose fame and fashion have passed away."

For ages before and up to the period of the Mohammedan invasion of India in the eleventh century, there were twelve great and specially holy Lingas in various parts of India. Some were destroyed during the Mohammedan conquest. One of them was the idol of Somnath, a block of stone four or five cubits high, and of proportionate thickness. Brahminical records refer it to the time of Krishna, implying an antiquity of 4,000 years. It is very probable that the worship of Siva, under the type of the Linga, prevailed throughout India as early as the fifth or sixth century of the Christian era; but phallic worship existed from unknown time.

One of the forms in which the *Linga* worship appears is that of the Lingayets, Lingawants, or Jangamas, the essential characteristic of which is wearing the emblem on some part of the dress or person. The type is of small size, made of copper or silver, and is commonly worn suspended in a case round the neck, or in the turban. The morning devotions of the worshippers of the

Linga, as an emblem of Siva, is thus described by Dr.
Duff in his *India and Indian Missions* :—" After ascend-
ing from the waters of the river, they distribute themselves along the muddy banks. Each then takes up a
portion of clay, and beginning to mould it into the form
of the Lingam, devoutly says, ' Reverence to Hara (a
name of Siva), I take this lump of clay ;' next addressing
the clay, he says, ' Siva, I make thy image.' The linga
being now formed, he presents to it water from the
Ganges, and various offerings. He then worships, rehearsing the names and attributes of the god ; and offers
flowers all round the image, commencing from the east ;
—adding : ' Receive, O Siva, these offerings of flowers.
Thus do I worship thee.' Again and again he worships
and bows. He last of all throws the flowers into the
water, prays to Siva to grant him temporal favours and
blessings ; twines his fingers one into the other ; places
the image once more before him ; and then flings it
away."

There is no country in the world where they pray
more than in Tibet. An ejaculatory prayer of six syl-
lables is continually on the lips of all the inhabitants of
that country. The shepherd repeats it in tending his
flocks, the merchant in awaiting a purchaser, the women
when engaged in household affairs. It is a sort of *ave
maria* or repetition of the talismanic words :—" Om mani
padmi oum," *Oh* (Lord) *the jewel in the lotus.* It is of
Hindu origin, and in India it could have had no other source
than in the worship of Siva. " In fact," says M. Michel
Nicolas, " it represents a symbol of Siva, the *lingam* in the
yoni, that is to say, the union of the male and female principle. With the adorers of Siva, the *mani* (the jewel) is one

of the most usual names of the lingam, and the *yoni* is represented by the *padmi* (lotus). This formula is, in its most primitive sense, an invocation to the universal creative energy, which is here represented under a symbol much used in the worship of Siva. It is absolutely foreign to Buddhism, as well with regard to the idea it expresses, as with regard to the form under which this idea is represented; it was not introduced into it until the worship of Siva became blended, in Nepaul, with Buddhist ideas. But the simple devotees of the country of snow, and of the country of herbs, entertain no doubts on the origin, nor on the real meaning of that obscure formula, and are fully convinced that in reciting it they are invoking the celestial spirits."*

Worship and reverence were also paid to the Phallus and Kteis among the Greeks and Romans.

According to Herodotus and Diodorus Siculus, the worship of Bacchus was imported into Greece by Melampus. "It was he," Herodotus says, " who taught the Greeks the name of Bacchus, the ceremonies of his worship, and who introduced among them the procession of the phallus." "Nothing is more simple," are Plutarch's words, "than the manner in which they celebrated formerly, in my country, the Dionysiaca. Two men walked at the head of the procession; one carried an amphora of wine, the other a vine branch, a third dragged a goat; a fourth bore a basket of figs; a figure of a phallus closed the procession."

There was a class of actors called phallophori and ithyphalli, who appeared in the procession of the Dionysiaca. The first bore long poles surmounted by the

* Boudin.

phallus, and crowned with violets and ivy. They walked along, repeating obscene songs, called φαλλικὰ ᾄσματα. The latter had their heads covered with wreaths, their hands full of flowers, and pretended to be drunk. They bore on their waistband large phalli made of wood or leather.

In the basket carried on the head of the Canephori in the Dionysiac processions, among other symbols was the phallus. One of the personages of the comedy of the Acharnians says (v. 242), "Advance canephoros, and let Xanthias (the slave), place the phallus erect." A hymn was then sung, which Aristophanes calls *phallic.* The Greeks usually represented the phallus alone, as a direct symbol, the meaning of which seems to have been among the last discoveries revealed to the initiated. It was the same, in emblematical writing, as the Orphic epithet, ΠΑΓΓΕΝΕΤΩΡ, *universal generator.**

That which the mysteries of Eleusis, Tertullian says, consider as most holy, that which is concealed with most care, what they are admitted to the knowledge of only at the latest moment, what the ministers of religion called epoptæ, excite the most ardent desire for, is the image of the virile member.

Dr. Schliemann gives a figure of a phallus of white marble in his *Troja,* page 173, found in the ruins of the second city.

In Rome, in the month of April, when the fertilising powers of nature begin to operate, and its productive powers to be visibly developed, a festival in honour of Venus took place; in it the phallus was carried in a cart, and led in procession by the Roman ladies to the temple

* Payne Knight.

of Venus outside the Colline gate, and then presented by them to the sexual part of the goddess.

The special time for the erection and worship of the phallus was the spring, as we learn from a passage of *Iamblichus De Mysteriis* :—" We say the erection of the phalli is a certain sign of prolific power, which, through this, is called forth to the generative energy of the world, on which account many phalli are consecrated in the spring, because then the whole world receives from the gods the power which is productive of all generation." *

At Lavinium, they carried in the streets, every day, during a month, a phallus remarkable for its proportions. The grossest expressions were then used on all sides ; a mother of one of the most distinguished families of the city had to place a crown on this obscene image. At last the disorder reached such a pitch that it attracted the attention of the Roman Senate in the year 567.

The Romans named Mutinus or Tutinus, the isolated phallus, and Priapus, the phallus affixed to a Hermes.

The Roman ladies offered publicly wreaths to Priapus, and they hung them on the phallus of the divinity.

The kteis or female organ, as the symbol of the passive or productive powers of nature, generally occurs on ancient Roman monuments, as the Concha Veneris, a Fig, Barley Corn, and the letter Delta.

The stone, which was brought from Phrygia, and which represented the great Mother Goddess Cybele, resembled a *vulva*, for it represented the *kteis*—that is to say, the female organ. "In other words," writes M. G. du Mousseaux, "it reproduced one of the types,

* *Taylor's Trans.*, page 53.

by the image of which the ancients represented the Goddess Nature."

In the Thesmophoria, the kteis was the object of public veneration, according to Sainte Croix. (*Mystères du Paganisme*, vol. ii., p. 13.)

Among the German and Scandinavian nations, the god Fricco corresponds to the Priapus of the Romans. Among the Saxons, he was adored under the form of a phallus.

In his ecclesiastical history of the North, Adam de Brome speaks of a temple at Upsala, in Sweden, in which the god Fricco was represented with an enormous phallus.

In Spain, Priapus was worshipped under the name of Hortanes, and in the ancient Nebrissa, the modern Lebrixa, a town of Andalusia, his worship was established. "The inhabitants of Nebrissa," says Silius Italicus, "celebrate the orgies of Bacchus. Light satyrs and bacchantes, covered with the sacred skin, are to be seen there, carrying during the nocturnal ceremonies the statue of Bacchus Hortanes." (See *Bello Punico I.*, v. 395.)

This worship has been found in different parts of America, in Mexico, Peru, Chili, at Hayti. In the Libri collection, sold some years ago at Sotheby's, was a statuette in solid gold from Mexico. It was thus described in the catalogue:—"The lower portion is very singular, being Phallic, and may therefore be meant as a representation of an aboriginal deity similar to the Priapus of ancient mythology. It is two inches (five centimètres) in height, and weighs about seven-eighths of an ounce." According to Mr. Stephens, the upright pillar in front of the temples of Yucatan is a phallus. At Copan are several monoliths, or phallic pillars, some of them in a rough state, and others sculptured; on one of the latter are carved emblems relative to uterine existence, parturition, etc. In Panuco was found in the temple a phallus, and in bas-relief in public places were deposited the sacred *membra conjuncta in coitu.* There were also similar symbols in Tlascala. We read in an ancient document, written by one of the companions of Fernando Cortez :—" In certain countries, and particularly at Panuco, they adore the phallus (il membro che portano gli uomini fra le gambe), and it is preserved in the temples." The inhabitants of Tlascala also paid worship to the sexual organs of a man and woman. In Peru several representations in clay of the phallus are met with. Juan de Batangos, in his *History of the Incas,* an unpublished manuscript in the library of the Escurial, says that " in the centre of the great square or court of the temple of the Sun, at Cuzco, was a column or pillar of stone, of the shape of a loaf of sugar, pointed at the top, and covered with gold leaf." * In Chili rude phallic figures are found of silver or of gold. At Hayti, according to M. Artaud, phalli have been discovered in different parts of the island, and are believed to be undoubtedly the manufacture of the original inhabitants of the island. At Honduras is an " idol of round stone" with two faces, representing the Lord of Life, which the Indians adore, offering blood procured from the prepuce. The Abbé de Bourbourg, who made careful explorations in Mexico and Central America, confirms these statements in regard to the Phallic symbolism in these countries.

It is probable that the mound-builders of North-

* Squier's *Serpent Symbol,* p. 50.

America were votaries of the same worship. Professor Troost has procured several images in Smith country, Tennessee, one of which was endowed disproportionately, like a Pan, or the idol at Lampsacus. Dr. Ramsay, of Knoxville, also describes two phallic simulacra in his possession, twelve and fifteen inches in length. The shorter one was of amphibolic rock, and so very hard that steel could make no impression upon it.

In one of the Marianne Islands, of the Pacific Ocean, on festive occasions a phallus, highly ornamented, called by the natives Tinas, is carried in procession. Phallic figures are of frequent occurrence in New Zealand. In Carl Bock's work on *Borneo*, p. 232, a Phallic figure is represented in almost the identical position of the god Khem in Egypt. " The phallic idea," writes Mr. Bonwick, " so strongly represented in every other part of the world as the type of creative force, was not unknown in Tasmania and Australia."

There are numerous evidences that Phallic worship was retained to a late period in Modern Europe.

The following notices of Phallic worship in modern times are taken from Boudin on *Phallic Worship.*

In Germany, the worship of Priapus was maintained even as late as the 12th century.

The inhabitants of Slavonia still following, in the 12th century, pagan customs, paid worship to Priapus, under the name of Pripe-gala. This people, who were hostile to their neighbours, who had embraced Christianity, made frequent incursions into the dioceses of Magdeburg and Sax. Several Saxon princes united, about the year 1110, to implore assistance from the neighbouring powers. They wrote to the prelates of Germany, of

Lorraine, and of France, and laid before them the deplorable situation in which the hate of these idolators had plunged them. " Every time," they said, " that these fanatics assembled to celebrate their religious ceremonies, they announce that their god Pripe-gala is, according to them, the same as Priapus, or the indecent Belphegor. When they have cut off some Christians' heads, before the profane altar of their god, they utter most terrible howls and cry out : 'Let us rejoice to-day, Christ is vanquished, and our invincible Pripe-gala is his conqueror.' "

In France, a document entitled *Sacerdotal Judgments on Crimes,* which seems to be of the 8th century, contains the following :—" If any one performs enchantments before the *fascinum,* let him do penance on bread and water during three lents."

The Council of Chalons, held in the 9th century, forbids this custom, inflicts punishment on whoever performs it, and thus attests its existence at that period. Burchard, who lived in the 12th century, gives the article of this Council in the following words :—" If any one performs incantations before the fascinum, he shall do penance on bread and water during three lents."

The Synodal Statutes of the Church of Mans, which are of the year 1247, inflicts the same punishment on whoever " had sinned before the fascinum." In the 14th century the Synodal Statutes of the Church of Tours, of the year 1396, forbid these acts. These statutes were then translated into French, and the word " fascinum " is there explained by that of " fesne :" " If any one performs any incantations before the fesne." . . .

In the Journal of Henry III. by L'Estoile, we read the following :—" In the same way the institutors of our ceremonies have had no shame of the most ancient pieces of antiquity, for the god of gardens has been adored in so many parts of France. Witness Saint Foutin, of Varailles, in Provence, to whom are dedicated the privy parts of either sex in wax. The ceiling of the chapel is covered with them, and when the wind agitates them, it sometimes disturbs one's devotions in honour of the saint. I was greatly scandalized, when I passed through that place, to hear several men named Foutin; the daughter of my hostess had a god-mother, a lady of the name of Foutine. When the Huguenots took Embrun, they found among the relics of the principal church a Priapus, of three pieces in the ancient fashion, the top of which was worn away from being constantly washed with wine: the women made a Saint Vinaigre of it, to be applied to a very strange use. When the men of Orange (the Huguenots) ruined the temple of St. Eutropius, they found a similar piece of sculpture, but coarser, covered with a skin and hair; it was publicly burnt in the square by the heretics, who were near being suffocated from the stench from it, through a miracle and punishment of the saint. There is another Saint Foutin in the town of Auxerre. Another in a town called Verdre, in Bourbonnais. There is another Saint Foutin in Bas Languedoc, in the diocese of Viviers, called Saint Foutin de Cines, and another at Posigny, to whom women have recourse when with child, or in order to have children."

At Saintes, women and children of both sexes carried in a certain procession, at the end of a blessed branch, a

loaf of bread, in the shape of a phallus. The name of
this loaf is in harmony with its shape, which reveals its
origin, and leaves no doubt as to the object it represents.

At St. Jean d'Angely, at Corpus Christi, loaves of
bread called ' fateaux,' and in the form of a phallus, were
carried in procession. This custom was still practised
when M. Maillard was sous-prefet of that town ; he had
it suppressed.

" They still show, at Antwerp," says Goropius, " a small
statue, formerly provided with a phallus, which decency
caused to be removed. This statue is placed over a door
near the public prison." According to this author,
Priapus had at Antwerp a very celebrated temple.
Goropius even quotes an opinion which derives the name
of the city of Antwerp from the Latin word *verpus*,
which expresses what the phallus represents.

In the town of Trani, not long ago, an old statue of
wood was carried in procession, during the Carnival,
which represented a complete Priapus in its ancient
proportions, that is to say, that the feature which distinguished the god was greatly out of proportion with
the rest of the body of the idol; it rose nearly as high
as its chin. The inhabitants of the country named this
figure " il santo membro."

The raising of the May Pole is a custom of Phallic
origin, and is typical of the fructifying powers of
Spring.

Among the simple and primitive races of men, the act
of generation was considered as no more than one of
the operations of nature contributing to the reproduction
of the species, as in agriculture the sowing of seed for

the production of corn,* and was consequently looked
upon as a solemn duty consecrated to the Deity; as
Payne Knight remarks, "it was considered as a solemn
sacrament in honour of the Creator."

In those early days, all the operations of nature were
consecrated to some divinity from whom they were supposed to emanate; thus the sowing of seed was presided
over by Ceres.

In Egypt, the act of generation was consecrated to
Khem, in Assyria to Vul, in India to Siva; in Greece, in
the primitive pastoral age, to Pan, and in later times to
Priapus, and in Italy to Mutinus. Among the Mexicans,
the god of generation was named Triazoltenti. These
gods became the representatives of the generative or
fructifying powers in man and nature.

"Hevia," writes General Forlong,† "is equivalent to
Zoe life, from the Greek to live; thus what is called
'the fall,' ascribed to Eva, or Hevia the female, and
Adam the male, becomes in reality the acts connected
with generation, conception, and production, and the destruction of virginity.—Adam 'fell' from listening to
Eve, and she from the serpent tempting her,—details
which merely assure us that we have procreative acts in
all stories regarding Hawa (in Hindustani Lust, Wind,
Air-Juno) and Chavah or Eve, or as the Arabs call it,
Hayyat, life or creation. Eating forbidden fruit was
simply a figurative mode of expressing the performance of
the act necessary for the perpetuation of the human
race."

The following curious passage from *Cook's First Voyage*

---

* In Greek φυτεύω means to plant seeds and to generate.

† *Rivers of Life*, vol. i., p. 142.

will show the reverence with which the procreative act was looked upon by a primitive race in the islands of the Pacific Ocean; it was considered a religious duty:—" On the 14th I directed that divine service should be performed at the fort: we were desirous that some of the principal Indians should be present, but when the hour came, most of them returned home. Mr. Banks, however, crossed the river, and brought back Tubourai Tamaide and his wife Tonio, hoping that it would give occasion to some inquiries on their part, and some instruction on ours: having seated them, he placed himself between them, and during the whole service they very attentively observed his behaviour, and very exactly imitated it; standing, sitting, or kneeling, as they saw him do; they were conscious that we were employed about something serious and important, as appeared by their calling to the Indians without the fort to be silent; yet when the service was over, neither of them asked any questions, nor would they attend to any attempt that was made to explain what had been done.

" Such were our matins; our Indians thought fit to perform vespers of a different kind. A young man, near six feet high, performed the rites of Venus with a little girl, about eleven or twelve years of age, before several of our people and a great number of the natives; but, as appeared, in perfect conformity to the custom of the place. Among the spectators were several women of superior rank, particularly Oberea, who may properly be said to have assisted at the ceremony, for they gave instruction to the girl how to perform her part." *

* *Cook's First Voyage*, Hawkesworth, ii., 128.

This account of the procreative ceremony among the Otaheitans has been further described by Voltaire in his story, *Les Oreilles du Comte de Chesterfield*, with additional circumstances :—" The Princess Obeira, queen of the island of Otaheite, after having made us many presents with a politeness worthy of a queen of England, was anxious to be present some morning at our English service. We celebrated it with as much ceremony as possible. She invited us to her's after dinner ; it was on the 14th of May, 1769. We found her surrounded by about a thousand persons of both sexes, ranged in a semi-circle, and in respectful silence. A very pretty young girl, slightly dressed, was lying on a raised bench, which served as an altar. The Queen Obeira ordered a handsome young man of about twenty to go and sacrifice. He uttered a kind of prayer, and ascended the altar. The two sacrificers were half naked. The queen, with a majestic air, taught the young victim the most proper manner to consummate the sacrifice. All the Otaheitans were so attentive and so respectful, that none of our sailors dared to interrupt the ceremony by an indecent laugh. This is what I have seen, it is for you to draw inferences."

" This sacred festival does not astonish me," said Dr. Goodman, " I feel persuaded that this was the first festival that men ever celebrated, and I do not see why we should not pray to God when we are going to procreate a being in his image, as we pray before we take our food, which serves to support our body ; working to give birth to a reasonable being, is a most noble and holy action : as thus the first Indians thought who revered the Lingam, the symbol of generation ; the ancient

Egyptians who carried the phallus in procession; the Greeks who erected temples to Priapus."

Three phases in the representation of the phallus should be distinguished; first, when it was the object of reverence and religious worship; secondly, when it was used as a protecting power against evil influences of various kinds, and as a charm or amulet against envy or the evil eye; there are numerous instances of its use for this purpose. It appears on the lintel of a postern gate at Alatri, in a baker's shop at Pompeii, on the wall at Fiesole, on the walls of Grotta Torre, on the walls of Todi; on the doors of tombs at Palazzuolo, at Castel di Asro in Etruria. The phallus also frequently occurs on amulets of porcelain found in Egypt, and of bronze in Italy. These were usually worn round the neck. The bust of a woman was found at Pompeii with a necklace of eight phalli round her neck. In Dyer's *Pompeii*, p. 447, is figured a necklace of amulets with two phalli found on a female skeleton. Phalli were also frequently placed in vineyards and gardens to scare away thieves. Thirdly, when it was the result of mere licentiousness and dissolute morals. This phase we need not further notice, as it is completely outside our purpose.

Another cause also contributed to the reverence and frequent representations of the phallus—the natural desire of women among all races, barbarous as well as civilized, to be the fruitful mother of children—especially as, among some people, women were esteemed according to the number of children they bore; and as, among the Mohammedans of the present day, it is sinful not to contribute to the population; as a symbol, therefore, of prolificacy, and as the bestower of offspring, the phallus

became an object of reverence, and especial reverence
among women. At Pompeii was found a gold ring,
with the representation of a phallus on its bezel, supposed
to have been worn by a barren woman. To propitiate
the deity, and to obtain offspring, offerings of this symbol
were made in Roman temples by women, and this custom
has been retained in modern times at Isernia, near Naples.
Stone offerings of phalli are also made at the present day
in a Buddhist temple in Pekin, and for the same object
Mohammedan women kiss with reverence the organ of
generation of an idiot or saint. In India this worship has
found its most extensive development. There young girls
who are anxious for husbands, and married women who
are desirous of progeny, are ardent worshippers of Siva,
and his symbol, the lingam, which is frequently wreathed
with flowers by his female worshippers, is exhibited in
enormous proportions.

In the 16th century St. Foutin in the south of France,
St. Ters at Antwerp, and in the last century Saints
Cosmo and Damiano at Isernia, near Naples, were worshipped for the same purpose by young girls and barren
women. Wax phalli were offered to these saints, and
placed on their altar. Sir William Hamilton and Mr.
Payne Knight were led to investigate the origin of the
ceremony. The results of their inquiries left no doubt
that it was a remnant of the worship of Priapus, which
appears to have lingered on this spot without interruption
from pagan times.

According to Henry Stephens, Priapus was worshipped
at Bourg-Dun, near Bourges. Barren women performed
a *novena* there; and on each of the nine days they
stretched themselves over the figure of the saint, which

was placed horizontally. They then scraped, according to Dulaure, a certain part of Saint Guerlichon, which was as prominent as that of Priapus; what they scraped off, mixed with water, formed a miraculous draught. Henry Stephens adds, " I do not know if the saint is in similar credit at the present day, for those who have seen it say that for the last twelve years it has had that part worn away from continually scraping it."

In France, in the last century, a belief in the efficacy of some saints for a similar purpose was retained. The following extract is from a work published in 1797 : —" At the further end of the Port of Brest, beyond the fortifications, there was a small chapel, and in this chapel was a statue honoured with the name of saint. If decency permitted me to describe Priapus with his attributes, I should depict that statue. Barren women, or those who feared to be so, went to this statue, and after having scraped what I dare not mention, and having drunk the powder infused in a glass of water from a fountain, they took their departure, with the hope of becoming fruitful."

According to M. Pastureaux, quoted by Dulaure, there was at Bourges, rue Chevriere, " a small statue placed in the wall of a house, the sexual organs of which were worn away from being continually scraped by women, who swallowed what they scraped off, in the hope of becoming fruitful; this statue is in the country named the ' good Saint Greluchon ' (le bon Saint Greluchon)."

Sir Gardner Wilkinson records similar superstitious beliefs at the present day at Ekhmim, in Egypt. The superstitions of the natives here ascribed the same properties to a stone in one of the sheikh's tombs, and like-

wise to that of the temple of Pan, which the statues of
the god of generation, the patron deity of Panoplis (Ekhmim), were formerly believed to have possessed; the
modern women of Ekhmim, with similar hopes and equal
credulity, offer their vows to these relics for a numerous
progeny.

Dr. Sinclair Coghill, now of Ventnor, who has travelled
extensively in China and Japan, has kindly contributed
the following, recording his experiences of similar superstitious beliefs and practices in India and Japan at the
present day :—

"On my way out to the Far East, in 1861, I had an
opportunity of visiting the great cave temple of Elephanta,
near Bombay. In each of the monolithic chapels within
the area of the main temple, I observed a gigantic stone
phallus projecting from the centre of the floor. The emblem was in some cases wreathed with flowers, while
the floor was strewed with the faded chaplets of the
fair devotees, some of whom at the time of my visit,
fancying themselves unobserved, were invoking the subtle
influence of the stony charm by rubbing their pudenda
against its unsympathetic surface, while muttering their
prayers for conjugal love, or for maternal joy, as the need
might be.

"In the course of two visits I paid to Japan, in 1864
and in 1869, I was very much struck with the extent to
which this ancient symbolic worship had survived through
many phases of rational religion, and was still attracting
numerous devotees to its shrines. I visited a large
temple devoted to this cultus in a small island off Ka-
matura, the ancient and now deserted capital of Japan,
in the Bay of Yokohama, some miles below the Foreign

Settlements. The temple 'Timbo,' as the Japanese term such places of worship, covered a large extent of ground. The male symbol was the only object of veneration apparently; in various sizes, some quite colossal, and more or less faithfully modelled from nature, it held the sole place of honour on the altars in the principal hall and subsidiary chapels of the temple. Before each the fair devotees might be seen fervently addressing their petitions, and laying upright on the altar, already thickly studded with similar oblations, a votive phallus, either of plain wrought cut wood from the surrounding grove, or of other more elaborately prepared materials. I also remarked some of them handing to the presiding priests pledgets of the luxurious silk tissue paper of Japan, previously applied to the genitals, which, with a muttered invocation, were burned in a large censer before the phallic idol. I was much struck with the earnestness with which the whole of the proceedings were conducted, and with the strong hold which this most ancient religious cultus still evidently retained over the minds of a people otherwise remarkable for the mobility of their opinions and manners.

"The present religions most prevalent in Japan are the Sintoo and the Buddhist. The Sintoo, the more ancient religion of the people, consists of a multiple personification of the powers of nature, and of localities, mountains, streams, etc., closely resembling the classical mythology of ancient Greece and Rome. This ancient worship has been revived to a great extent lately by the old conservative party, who succeeded in restoring the line of the Mikados to actual sovereignty by the revolution of 1868, which overthrew the dynasty of the Tycoons. This revival has been made greatly to the detriment of the Buddhist faith, which, more recently imported as a literary product from China, held principal sway in the large cities, and among the *literati*. The Phallic cultus still prevailing in the remoter country districts is probably a surviving relic of an earlier phase of the Sintoo religion in which the phallic element is still represented. In travelling in Japan, I have seen again and again on the Tokaido, or public road, a hedged recess, in which was implanted on its pedestal a gigantic stone phallus of most unequivocal character. The whole population of the country seem so habituated to the symbol as to regard it apart from its more material or grosser suggestion. I have seen a prodigious representation of the male organ, modelled in colour, borne erect by priests on a platform through the principal streets of Nagasaki, without attracting anything but respectful notice from the seething crowd."

The following passage from Captain Burton's *Dahomé* exhibits similar customs among a rude and barbarous people of the present day :—" Among all barbarians whose primal want is progeny, we observe a greater or less development of the Phallic worship. In Dahomé it is uncomfortably prominent. Every street from Whydah to the capital is adorned with the symbol, and the old ones are not removed. The Dahoman Priapus is a clay figure, of any size between a giant and a pigmy, crouched upon the ground, as if contemplating its own attributes. The head is sometimes a wooden block rudely carved, more often dried mud, and the eyes and teeth are supplied by cowries. The tree of life is anointed with palm oil, which drops into a pot or shard placed below it, and the would-be mother of children prays that the great god Legba will make her fertile."

Mr. H. H. Johnston notes a similar worship in Congo. " On the Lower Congo, as far as Stanley Pool, phallic worship in various forms prevails. It is not associated with any rites that might be called particularly obscene; and on the coast, where manners and morals are particularly corrupt, the phallus cult is no longer met with. In the forests between Manyanga and Stanley Pool it is not rare to come upon a little rustic temple, made of palm-fronds and poles, within which male and female figures, nearly or quite life size, may be seen, with disproportionate genital organs, the figures being intended to represent the male and female principle. Around these carved and painted statues are many offerings of plates, knives and cloth, and frequently also the phallic symbol may be seen dangling from the rafters. There is not the slightest suspicion of obscenity in all this, and any one qualifying this worship of the generative power as obscene does so hastily and ignorantly. It is a solemn mystery to the Congo native, a force but dimly understood, and, like all mysterious natural manifestations, it is a power that must be propitiated and persuaded to his good."*

The reverence as well as worship paid to the phallus, in early and primitive days, had nothing in it which partook of indecency; all ideas connected with it were of a reverential and religious kind. When Abraham, as mentioned in Genesis, in asking his servant to take a solemn oath, makes him lay his hand on his parts of generation (in the common version " under his thigh"),

* H. H. Johnston, *The River Congo*, p. 405.

it was that he required, as a token of his sincerity, his
placing his hand on the most revered part of his body;
as at the present day a man would place his hand on his
heart in order to evince his sincerity. Jacob, when dying,
makes his son Joseph perform the same act. A similar
custom is still retained among the Arabs at the present
day. An Arab, in taking a solemn oath, will place his
hand on his virile member, in attestation of sincerity.*

The indecent ideas attached to the representation of
the phallus were, though it seems a paradox to say
so, the result of a more advanced civilization verging
towards its decline, as we have evidence at Rome and
Pompeii.†

" We must carefully distinguish," as M. Barrè writes,
" among these phallic representations, a religious side, and
a purely licentious side. These two classes correspond
with two different epochs of civilization, with two different
phases of the human mind. The generative power presented itself first as worthy of the adoration of men; it
was symbolized in the organs in which it is centred; and
then no licentious idea was mingled with the worship of
these sacred objects. If this spirit of purity became
weaker as civilization became more developed, as luxury
and vices increased, it still must have remained the peculiar
attribute of some simple minds : and hence we must consider under this point of view all objects in which nudity
is veiled, so to speak, under a religious motive. Let us
look upon those coarse representations with the same eye
with which the native population of Latium saw them, an
ignorant and rude population, and consequently still pure

---

* *Memoires sur l'Egypte*, partie deuxieme, p. 196.
† *Secret Museum of Naples*, London, 1871.

and virtuous, even in the most polished and most depraved times of the Empire; let us consider from this same point of view all those coarse statues of the god of gardens, those phalli and amulets; and let us recall to our minds that, even at the present day, the simple peasants of some parts of Italy are not completely cured of such super-stitions."

In this connection we may introduce an extremely just and apposite remark of Constant in his work on *Roman Poly-theism*:—" Indecent rites may be practised by a religious people with the greatest purity of heart. But when incredulity has gained a footing amongst these peoples, these rites become then the cause and pretext of the most revolting corruption." A similar remark has been made by Voltaire. Speaking of the worship of Priapus, he says : " Our ideas of propriety lead us to suppose that a ceremony which appears to us infamous could only be invented by licentiousness ; but it is impossible to believe that licentiousness and depravity of manners would ever have led among any people to the establishment of reli-gious ceremonies ; profligacy may have crept in in the lapse of time, but the original institution was always in-nocent and free from it ; the early *agapes,* in which boys and girls kissed one another modestly on the mouth, de-generated at last into secret meetings and licentiousness. It is, therefore, probable that this custom was first intro-duced in times of simplicity, that the first thought was to honour the Deity in the symbol of life which it has given us." In conclusion we may introduce the views of a recent French writer, Dr. Boudin, whose *Essay on Phallic Worship* is little known.

Modern historians have been strangely deceived, in Dr.

Boudin's opinion, in persisting in seeing in the Priapus
of antiquity, and in the Lingam of India, only a *symbol* of
generation. "Man does not adore *symbols*, and almost all
nations have adored Priapus; thousands of virgins have
sacrificed to Priapus and the Lingam the most precious
thing they possessed, and such sacrifices are not surely
offered to *symbols*. As well may we transform into *symbols*
the most obscure acts, of which the worship of the phallus
is, in reality, but the religious consecration."   And after
citing numerous instances of the worship of Priapus and
the reverence paid to the Phallus, he gives the following
as his conclusions on the subject of that worship:—

"In presence of the preceding facts, which attest one
of the most universally extended cults, or religious worships, what can we think of the opinion which persists
in seeing in the Priapus of antiquity and in the Lingam of
India only a symbol and an outline of generation?"

Man never attached the least importance to the phallus
issuing from the hand of the sculptor, a phallus assuredly
as symbolic as a consecrated phallus could be.   To be
the object of worship, the phallus required a previous
religious consecration, without which the Priapus and the
Lingam were nothing but a fragment of stone, but a piece
of wood—*inutile lignum*, as the Roman poet, Horace, says.

"In religione," says Iamblichus, "non potest fieri
opus ullum alicujus mirabilis efficaciæ, nisi adsit illic
superiorum aliquis spectator operis et *impletor*."

After the consecration, the scene changed; the wood,
inutile lignum, became a god; Deus inde, furum aviumque
maxima formido.

What has taken place?   Let us ask human nature, the
philosophers, the Fathers of the Church.   All answer

with one accord, that an incarnation of the Deity has taken place in the wood or in the stone.

This was the creed of antiquity; this is what modern India still believes. In the opinion of St. John Chrysostom statues are: λίθοι καὶ δαίμονες, stones and spirits of evil. In the opinion of St. Cyprian, the spirits are in the stone or under the stone: Hi ergo Impuri Spiritus sub statuis et imaginibus delitescunt. Minutius Felix expresses himself in somewhat similar terms. According to Tertullian, to make an idol was to make a body for a demon (*De Idolatria*).

Assuredly there is nothing in these quotations which authorise the interpretation of the present day considering them as symbols. Let us also cite Arnobius, who, before his conversion, had been a fervent adorer of these gods, and ought to be an authority on these forms of belief:—
"If I met," he says, "a stone anointed with oil (lapidem ex olivi unguine sordidatum—this is the consecration), I addressed it, I asked favours (affabar, beneficia poscebam) as if it had been inhabited by a power (tanquam inesset vis præsens)." In another place the same author, after having accused his former co-religionists of adoring statues, puts in their mouth this very legitimate objection:—"Error; we adore neither the bronze, nor the gold, nor the silver; but those whom a religious consecration (dedicatio sacra) renders the indwellers of the stone (efficit habitare simulacris)." It is also in allusion to the general belief in the power of the consecration of the stone, *dedicatio sacra*, that Lucian, always disposed to sneer at any religious idea which he meets, exclaims, "Every stone renders oracles (πᾶς λίθος χρησμῳδεῖ), provided it is anointed with holy oil."

Consecration.

"How," says Minutius Felix, "do they make a god? It is melted, it is struck, it is sculptured, it is not yet a god (nondum est deus), it is soldered, it is manufactured, it is raised erect; it is not yet a god (nondum est deus); lastly, it is adorned, it is *consecrated,* it is prayed to, it is now a god, when man has willed it, and has dedicated it (ornatur, consecratur, oratur, tunc postremo deus est, cum homo illum voluit et dedicavit)."

"In India," says Delafosse, " the lingam issuing from the hands of the workman is deemed an instrument without virtue; it acquires it only by consecration—that is to say, when a Brahmin has blessed it, and has rendered incarnate in it the deity by religious ceremonies." *

To sum up, the phallus, in the same manner as statues, plants, animals, objects of worship among nations, was only the outward covering, the receptacle, the vehicle of the deity which was supposed to be contained within it, a deity to which alone religious worship was paid. This outward covering, this receptacle, this vehicle, was varied in an infinity of modes with regard to its form, but it was neither a symbol nor an allegory.†

The Dionysia (Διονύσια) were celebrated in honour of Bacchus, Διόνυσος. The etymology of this word has been the subject of long discussions. The older opinion derived it from Ζεύς, genitive Διός, Jupiter or God, and

---

* *Essai Historique sur l'Inde.*

† On my writing to a learned friend to ask his opinion on this view, I received the following reply:—"The ancients worshipped the phallus—the yoni and the linga—because they worshipped nature powers in general. In that sense, no doubt, they were regarded as 'divine,' but it is hardly true that they regarded them 'as an incarnation of the deity.' "

from the name of the town of Nysa, where Bacchus was brought up. Some philologists versed in Indian languages derive it from DÉVA, which means god or king (king of Nysa); and it has been remarked that the epithet of DÊVANICHI, king of the town of Nicha (city of the night) has been given to Siva, who is the same as Bacchus.

These festivals were sometimes designated by the word ὄργια, which was also applied to the mysteries of the other gods; they were also called βακχεία. They were brought from Egypt into Greece by Melampus, the son of Amithaon, and the Athenians celebrated them with more pomp than the other Greeks. The principal archon (ἐπώνυμος) presided over them, and the priests who celebrated the religious rites occupied the first places in the theatre, and in the public assemblies. Originally these festivals exhibited neither extravagance nor splendour; they were simply devoted to joy and pleasure within the houses. All public ceremonies were confined to a procession, in which there appeared a vasefull of wine, and wreathed with vine leaves; a goat, a basket of figs, and the phalli. At a later period this procession was celebrated with greater pomp; the number of priests of Bacchus increased. Those who took part in the procession were suitably dressed, and sought by their gestures to represent some of the customs which Faith attributed to the god of wine. They dressed themselves in fawn skins. They wore on their head a mitre, and they carried in their hand a thyrsus, a tympanum or·a flute. Their heads were wreathed with ivy, vine leaves, and pine branches. Some imitated the dress and fantastic postures of Silenus, of Pan, and the Satyrs; they covered their legs with goat skins, and carried the horns of animals; they rode on asses, and dragged after them goats intended to be sacrificed. In the town this frenzied crowd was followed by priests carrying sacred vases, the first of which was filled with water; then followed young girls selected from the most distinguished families, and called Canephori (κανηφόροι), because they bore small baskets of gold full of all sorts of fruits, of cakes, and of salt; but the principal object among these, according to St. Croix, was the phallus, made of the wood of a fig-tree. (In the comedy of the *Acharnians*, by Aristophanes, one of the characters in the play says,—" Come forward a little, Canephoros, and you, Xanthias, slave, place the phallus erect.")

After these came the periphallia (περιφαλλία), a troop of men who carried long poles with phalli hung at the end of them: they were crowned with violets and ivy, and as they walked they repeated obscene songs called φαλλικὰ ᾄσματα. These men were called phallophori (φαλλοφόροι); these must not be confounded with the ithyphalli (ἰθύφαλλοι), who, in an indecent dress, and sometimes in a woman's dress, their head covered with garlands, their hands full of flowers, and pretending to be drunk, wore at their waistband monstrous phalli made of wood or leather: among the ithyphalli, must also be counted those who assumed the costume of Pan, or of the Satyrs. There were other persons, called licnophori (λικνόφοροι), who had the care of the mystic winnowing-fan, an emblem the presence of which was considered as indispensable in these kinds of festivals. It was on account of this symbol that the epithet licnite (λικνίτης) was given to Bacchus.

Outside the town, the more respectable persons, the matrons and modest virgins, separated themselves from the procession. But the people, the countless multitude of Sileni, of Satyrs, and of nymph bacchantes, spread themselves over the open spaces and the valleys, stopped in solitary places to get up dances or to celebrate some festival, making the rocks re-echo with the sound of drums and flutes, and more especially with cries constantly repeated, by which they invoked the god : "Évohé Sabœe! Évohé Bacche! O Iacche! Io Bacche!" Εὐοῖ Σάβοῖ, Εὐοῖ Βάκχε ὦ "Ιακχε, 'Ιὼ βάκχε. The first of these words recalls the words with which Jupiter encouraged Bacchus when, in the war of the giants, the latter defended the throne of his father : "εὖ υἰὲ, εὖ υἰὲ Βάκχε," called out the master of the gods : they added also "ὖης ἄττης ; ἄττης ὖης."

The description we have given was chiefly applied to the greater Dionysia (μεγάλα), or to the new Dionysia (νεώτερα) ; there were six other festivals of this name, the ceremonies of which must have borne some resemblance to that already described. There were, in the first place, the ancient Dionysia (ἀρχαιότερα), which were celebrated at Limnæ, and in which appeared fourteen priestesses called Geræræ (Γέραιραι, venerable) who, before entering on their duties, swore that they were pure and chaste. There were the lesser Dionysia (μικρά), which were celebrated in the autumn, and in the country ; the Brauronia (Βραυρώνια) of Brauron, a village of Attica ; the Nyctelia (νυκτήλια), the mysteries of which it was forbidden to reveal ; the Theoina (θέοινα) ; the Lenean (ληναῖα), festivals of the wine-press (ληνός) ; the Omophagia (ὠμοφαγία) in honour of Bacchus car-

nivorous (ὠμοφάγος), to whom formerly human victims
were offered, and whose priests ate raw meat; the
Arcadian ('Αρκαδικὰ), which were celebrated in Arcadia
by dramatic contests; and lastly the Trieterica (τριετηρικὰ),
which were celebrated every three years in memory of the
period during which Bacchus made his expedition in
India.

The Bacchic mysteries and orgies are said to have been
introduced from Southern Italy into Etruria, and from
thence to Rome.   Originally they were only celebrated
by women, but afterwards men were admitted, and their
presence led to the greatest disorders.   In these festivals
the phallus played a prominent part, and was publicly exhibited.   At Lavinium the festival lasted a month, during
which time a phallus, remarkable for its proportions, was
carried each day through the streets.   The coarsest language was heard on all sides; a matron of one of the
most considerable families in the town placed a wreath
on this obscene image.

Pacula Annia, pretending to act under the inspiration of Bacchus, ordered that the Bacchanalia should be
held during five days in every month.   It was from the
time that these orgies were carried on after this new
plan that, according to the statement of an eye-witness
(Liv. xxxix. 13), licentiousness and crimes of every description were committed.

This was carried to such an excess that the Senate
in 186 B.C. issued a decree to suppress and prohibit
these festivals; it was ordered that no Bacchanalia
should be held in Rome or in Italy.

Our task is now ended.   We have traced the spon-
taneous and independent development in many countries

of the worship, the reverence paid by man to the generative power, that reproductive force which pervades all nature. To the primitive man it was the most mysterious of all manifestations. The visible physical powers of nature—the sun, the sky, the storm—naturally claimed his reverence, but to him the generative power was the most mysterious of all powers. In the vegetable world, the live seed placed in the ground, and hence germinating, sprouting up, and becoming a beautiful and umbrageous tree, was a mystery. In the animal world, as the cause of all life, by which all beings came into existence, this power was a mystery. In the view of primitive man generation was the action of the Deity itself. It was the mode in which He brought all things into existence, the sun, the moon, the stars, the world, man were generated by Him. To the productive power man was deeply indebted, for to it he owed the harvests and the flocks which supported his life ; hence it naturally became an object of reverence and worship.

Primitive man wants some object to worship, for an abstract idea is beyond his comprehension, hence a visible representation of the generative Deity was made, with the organs contributing to generation most prominent, and hence the organ itself became a symbol of the power.

As this power was visible through all nature and in all countries, similar ideas were suggested to man, and reverential worship to it became wide-spread among many nations and races.

E

THE EVIL EYE,

AND ITS CONNECTION WITH PHALLIC ILLUSTRATION.

THE belief in the Evil Eye is one of the most widely extended of superstitions; it crops out in the remotest corners of the globe. It is found among the intellectual Greeks and the cultivated Romans of the Augustan age as among the rudest savages.

If the universality of a belief were an argument for its truth, the doctrine which asserts the power of the Evil Eye would be above all controversy. Transmitted by uncounted generations, perhaps, to all the nationalities of the globe, the theory of fascination, which lies at the basis of all witchcraft, holds a place among the very first ideas formulated by mankind.

It takes its origin from that common but unamiable feeling in human nature, when an invidious glance or look of envy is cast on the happier lot or on the superior possessions of others. To avert the supposed effects of this glance of envy, this Evil Eye, recourse is had to the superstitious practice of using some attractive object or talisman to turn aside the baneful dart of the Evil Eye.

"The dreaded *invidia,*" as C. O. Müller writes, "according to the belief of antiquity, was with so much the greater certainty warded off the more repulsive, nay, disgusting, the object worn for that purpose; and the numberless Phallic images, although originally symbols of life-creating nature, had afterwards, however, only this meaning and aim." *

* *Ancient Art,* page 627.

A like stage of mental progress will lead to the manifestation of similar beliefs, of superstitions almost identically
the same. The mental stage being low, the ideas and
beliefs emanating from it will necessarily be rude and
coarse. Similar counter-agents also occur to ward off
the effects of a glance of envy from an evil eye. The
methods adopted for obviating its effects are of course
merely the offspring of fear acting on ignorance.

Many proofs may be adduced of the existence of this
belief, and of similar means to avert the effects of the
Evil Eye, not only among the ancient Greeks and Romans,
but also throughout Europe, Asia, Africa, and America
at the present day.

It is wide spread all over the world, from China to
Peru. The Greek of the present day entertains the
same horror of the *kako-mats* as his ancestors did of the
βάσκινος ὀφθαλμός, and the *mal occhio* of modern Italy is the
traditional *fascinatio* of the Romans. The inhabitants of
Malabar and the Hindoos, like the Turks and Arabians,
apologise for the possession of jewels with which they deco-
rate their children on the plea that they are intended to
draw aside the Evil Eye; the Mahometans suspend objects
from the ceilings of their apartments for the same purpose,
and the object of the Singalese in placing those whitened
chatties on their gables is to divert the mysterious
influence from their dwellings. Amongst the Tamils at
Jafferabad the same belief prevails as amongst the Irish
and Scotch, that their cattle are liable to injury from the
blight of an evil eye, thus recalling the expression of
Virgil's shepherd, "Nescio quis teneros oculus mihi
fascinat agnos."

Whole populations have been said to be endowed with

the power of the Evil Eye : among the ancients the Telchines, the Triballi, the Thebans, the Illyrians, and all the Thracian women. Among the moderns it is attributed by the Christians to the Turks; to the Christians, whether Catholics, Greeks, or Armenians, by the Turks ; to the Sunnites by the Schiites, and to the Shiites by the Sunnites. In the mouth of the orthodox "Evil Eye" is a term of abuse against infidels, possessed as such by unclean spirits. Christian and Moslem agree to endow with it the Gipsies and the Jews, and sometimes the Hindoos.

De Farra narrates that at Marcati there are such sorcerers that they eat the inside of anybody only by fixing their eyes upon him. In the country of Sennaar and Fassold they have rivals not less powerful, who by a mere look of their evil eye (*ain el hafrid*) stop the blood in the heart and the arteries of their enemy, desecrate his entrails, unsettle his intellect. The Sardinians have a saying amongst themselves : " *Deo si guardi d'occhio di litterato*" (May the Lord preserve you from being looked by a man of letters), for the ailments they inflict are much worse than those inflicted by other people.

The Romans attributed the Evil Eye to the late Pius IX. An Italian countess was turned out of Rome, as she was seen making the sign against the Evil Eye when the Pope was giving his blessing. An amusing story is also told of the late Pope, when saying prayers at the audience at the Vatican ; on coming to the passage in the Lord's Prayer, "Lead us not into temptation," he looked over towards a very ugly old lady, upon which the lady boldly repeated aloud, " Deliver us from the Evil Eye" (*Libera nos a malo-occhio*).

Mr. Barham Zincke tells us that "among the Egyptians

of the present day there is an universal belief in the noticing of the Evil Eye. If any one has looked upon an object with envious and covetous feelings evil will ensue; not, however—and this is the heart and peculiarity of the superstition—to the coveted or envied object. A mother in easy circumstances will keep her child in shabby clothes and begrimed with dirt in order that those who see it may not think it a beautiful object, and so cast an anxious or covetous eye upon it. Some conspicuous object is placed among the caparisons of a beautiful horse or camel, that the eye of the passer-by may be attracted to it, and so withdrawn from the horse or camel. The entire dress of a Nubian young lady consists of a fringe of shredded leather, two or three inches deep, worn round the loins. On the upper ridge of this fringe two or three bunches of small white cowries are fastened. The traveller might at first, and probably generally does, suppose that this is merely a piece of coquetry, inspired by the desire to attract attention. The truth is quite the reverse. The white shells against the ebon skin are, it is true, intended to attract attention—not at all, however, in the way of coquetry, but from the opposite wish, that the eye of the passer-by may be attracted to the shells, and thus the wearer may herself escape the effects of the evil-coveting eye."

Lord Lytton writes:—" This superstition still flourishes in Magna Græcia with scarcely diminished vigour. At Naples the superstition works well for the jewellers—so many charms and talismans do they sell for the ominous fascination of the *mal occhio!* In Pompeii the talismans were equally numerous, but not always of so elegant a shape nor of so decorous a character. But, generally

speaking, a coral ornament was, as it is now, among the
favourite averters of this evil influence. The Thebans
about Pontus were supposed to have an hereditary claim
to this charming attribute, and could even kill grown-up
men with a glance. As for Africa, where the belief also
still exists, certain families could not only destroy children,
but wither up trees; but they did not with curses, but
praises. The *malus oculus* was not always different from
the eyes of other people. But persons, especially of the
fairer sex, with double pupils to the organ, were above
all to be shunned and dreaded. The Illyrians were said
to possess this fatal deformity. In all countries, even in
the North, the eye has ever been held the chief seat of
fascination; but nowadays ladies with a single pupil
manage the work of destruction pretty easily. So much
do we improve upon our forefathers!"

Mr. Bonwick tells us "that the red hand, stamped on
walls to this day by the Arabs in Palestine, as a charm
against the Evil Eye, is recognised not only in India and
America but also in Australia and Tasmania."

One of the objects most generally used to avert the
Evil Eye in Egypt, Greece, and Italy was the representation of the phallus. In Egypt in ancient time it
was extensively used. Numbers of examples have been
found, particularly at Bubastis, belonging to the twenty-
second dynasty, about 600 B.C. Some represent beings
with a phallus of abnormal proportions; others are remarkable for their gross indecency. One of the earliest
of known examples of representations of the phallus as
an amulet against the evil is on the lintel of a gateway on
the ancient walls of Alatri: three phalli are represented
joined together so as to form a cross. The phallus occurs

also for the same purpose on the wall at Fiesoli, on the walls of Grotta Torre, of Todi, on the doors of tombs at Palazzuolo, at Castel di Asro in Etruria. For a similar reason the phallus was placed over the doors of Greek and Roman houses, and in the inside of the houses, to divert the thoughts of passers-by, so that they might not look with an eye of envy on the house. In the principle street of Pompeii it occurs over the door of a house, and also in a baker's shop. Bronze representations, of the phallus, either erect or quiescent, are frequently found in the South of Italy. They are also often found, among other objects, in the necklaces of ladies.

INDEX.

A Selection

FROM

Mr. Redway's Publications.

GEORGE REDWAY,

15, YORK STREET, COVENT GARDEN, LONDON,

1886.

15, York Street, Covent Garden,

London, *January*, 1886.

Nearly ready.

Sultan Stork,

And other Stories, Sketches and Ballads.

BY

WILLIAM MAKEPEACE THACKERAY.

Now First Collected.

———

None of these pieces are included in the two recently published volumes issued by Messrs. Smith, Elder, and Co.

———

With an Appendix containing the Bibliography of Thackeray (first published in 1880), in a revised and enlarged form.

———

CONTENTS.

INTRODUCTION

I. PROSE.

1. **SULTAN STORK: being the One Thousand and Second Night.** By Major G. O'. G. Gahagan. [1842.]
2. **LITTLE SPITZ.** A Lenten Anecdote. [1841.]
3. **DICKENS IN FRANCE.** An Account of a French dramatic version of "Nicholas Nickleby," performed at a Paris theatre. [1842.]
4. **THE PARTIE FINE.** [1844.]
5. **ARABELLA; or, The Moral of the Partie Fine.** By Lancelot Wagstaff, Esq. [1844.]
6. **GOING TO SEE A MAN HANGED.** [1840.]
7. **UNPUBLISHED LETTER** (March, 1844) **TO THOMAS FRASER, OF** WHISTLE BINKIE.
8. **EXHIBITION GOSSIP.** [1842.]
9. **LETTERS ON THE FINE ARTS.** [1843.]
10. **PARIS CORRESPONDENCE.** [1833.]

II. VERSE.

11. **SATIRICAL VERSES** descriptive of (1) Louis Philippe; (2) Mr. Braham; (3) N. M. Rothschild, Esq.; (4) A. Bunn; (5) Sir Peter Laurie (Petrus Laureus). [1833.]
12. **LOVE IN FETTERS.** A Tottenham Court Road Ditty. [1833.]
13. **"DADDY, I'M HUNGRY."** Scene in an Irish Coachmaker's Family. [1843.]

THE BIBLIOGRAPHY OF THACKERAY. A Bibliographical List, arranged in chronological order, of the published Writings in Prose and Verse, and the Sketches and Drawings, of William Makepeace Thackeray (1829-1886). Revised and Enlarged.

———

GEORGE REDWAY, YORK STREET, COVENT GARDEN.

In crown 8vo., in French grey wrapper.   Price 6s.

A few copies on Large Paper.   Price 10s. 6d.

The Bibliography of Swinburne;

A BIBLIOGRAPHICAL LIST, ARRANGED IN CHRONOLOGICAL
ORDER, OF THE PUBLISHED WRITINGS
IN VERSE AND PROSE

OF

ALGERNON CHARLES SWINBURNE,

(1857-1884).

This Bibliography commences with the brief-lived *College Magazine*, to which Mr. SWINBURNE was one of the chief contributors when an undergraduate at Oxford in 1857-8. Besides a careful enumeration and description of the first editions of all his separately published volumes and pamphlets in verse and prose, the original appearance is duly noted of every poem, prose article, or letter, contributed to any journal or magazine (*e.g.*, *Once a Week*, *The Spectator*, *The Cornhill Magazine*, *The Morning Star*, *The Fortnightly Review*, *The Examiner*, *The Dark Blue*, *The Academy*, *The Athenæum*, *The Tatler*, *Belgravia*, *The Gentleman's Magazine*, *La République des Lettres*, *Le Rappel*, *The Glasgow University Magazine*, *The Daily Telegraph*, etc., etc.), whether collected or uncollected. Among other entries will be found a remarkable novel, published in instalments, and never issued in a separate form, and several productions in verse not generally known to be from Mr. SWINBURNE's pen. The whole forms a copious and it is believed approximately complete record of a remarkable and brilliant literary career, extending already over a quarter of a century.

₊ ONLY 250 COPIES PRINTED.

GEORGE REDWAY, YORK STREET, COVENT GARDEN.

HINTS TO COLLECTORS

OF ORIGINAL EDITIONS OF

THE WORKS OF

William Makepeace Thackeray.

BY

CHARLES PLUMPTRE JOHNSON.

Printed on hand-made paper and bound in vellum. Crown 8vo., 6s.

*The Edition is limited to five hundred and fifty copies,
twenty-five of which are on large paper.*

".... A guide to those who are great admirers of Thackeray, and are collecting first editions of his works. The dainty little volume, bound in parchment and printed on hand-made paper, is very concise and convenient in form; on each page is an exact copy of the title-page of the work mentioned thereon, a collation of pages and illustrations, useful hints on the differences in editions, with other matters indispensable to collectors. . . . . Altogether it represents a large amount of labour and experience."—*The Spectator.*

"Those who remember with pain having seen the original yellow backs o Thackeray's works knocked to pieces and neglected years ago, may be recommended to read Mr. C. P. Johnson's 'Hints to Collectors.'"—*The Saturday Review.*

".... Mr. Johnson has evidently done his work with so much loving care that we feel entire confidence in his statements. The prices that he has affixed in every case form a valuable feature of the volume, which has been produced in a manner worthy of its subject-matter."—*The Academy.*

"The list of works which Mr. Johnson supplies is likely to be of high interest to Thackeray collectors. His preliminary remarks go beyond this not very narrow circle, and have a value for all collectors of modern works."—*Notes and Queries.*

".... It is choicely printed at the Chiswick Press; and the author, Mr. Charles Plumptre Johnson, treats the subject with evident knowledge and enthusiasm. . . . It is not a Thackeray Bibliography, but a careful and minute description of the first issues, with full collations and statement of the probable cost. . . . Mr. Johnson addresses collectors, but is in addition a sincere admirer of the greatest satirist of the century."—*Book-Lore.*

".... This genuine contribution to the Bibliography of Thackeray will be invaluable to all collectors of the great novelist's works, and to all who treasure an 'editio princeps' the account here given of the titles and characteristics of the first issues will form a trustworthy guide. . . , The special features which will enable the purchaser at once to settle any question of authenticity in copies offered for sale are carefully collated."—*The Publisher's Circular.*

GEORGE REDWAY, YORK STREET, COVENT GARDEN.

HINTS TO COLLECTORS

OF ORIGINAL EDITIONS OF

THE WORKS OF

Charles Dickens.

BY

CHARLES PLUMPTRE JOHNSON.

Printed on hand-made paper, and bound in vellum.

Crown 8vo., 6s.

The Edition is limited to five hundred and fifty copies, fifty of which are on large paper.

"Enthusiastic admirers of Dickens are greatly beholden to Mr. C P. Johnson for his useful and interesting 'Hints to Collectors of Original Editions of the Works of Charles Dickens' (Redway). The book is a companion to the similar guide to collectors of Thackeray's first editions, is compiled with the like care, and produced with the like finish and taste."—*The Saturday Review.*

"This is a sister volume to the ' Hints to Collectors of First Editions of Thackeray,' which we noticed a month or two ago. The works of Dickens, with a few notable 'Dickensiana,' make up fifty-eight numbers . . . . and Mr. Johnson has further augmented the present volume with a list of thirty-six plays founded on Dickens's works, and another list of twenty-three published portraits of Dickens. As we are unable to detect any slips in his work, we must content ourselves with thanking him for the correctness of his annotations. It is unnecessary to repeat our praise of the elegant *format* of these books. . . . ."—*The Academy.*

"These two elegantly produced little books, printed on hand-made paper and bound in vellum, should be welcomed by the intending collector of the works of the two authors under treatment, and the more experienced bibliographer will find the verbatim reproductions of the original title-pages not without use. . . . . For the purpose of checking the correct numbers of these illustrations, verifying the collations, and detecting possible frauds . . . Mr. Johnson's books are unique. The ' Hints,' moreover, incorporated in his prefaces, . . . and the ' Notes' appended to each entry are serviceable, and often shrewd ; indeed, the whole labour, evidently one of love, bestowed upon the books is exceptionally accurate and commendable, and we hope to welcome Mr. Johnson at no distant date as a bibliographer of a more pretentious subject."—*Time.*

GEORGE REDWAY, YORK STREET, COVENT GARDEN.

In crown 8vo., 2 vols., cloth.   Price 6s.

The Valley of Sorek.

BY

GERTRUDE M. GEORGE.

With a Critical Introduction by RICHARD HERNE SHEPHERD.

" There is in the book a high and pure moral and a distinct conception of character. . . . The *dramatis personæ* . . . . are in reality strongly individual, and surprise one with their inconsistencies just as real human beings do. . . . There is something powerful in the way in which the reader is made to feel both the reality and the untrustworthiness of his (the hero's) religious fervour, and the character of the atheist, Graham, is not less strongly and definitely conceived. . . . It is a work that shows imagination and moral insight, and we shall look with much anticipation for another from the same hand."—*Contemporary Review.*

" The characters are clearly defined, the situations are strong, and the interest evoked by them is considerable. The women in particular are admirably drawn."—*Athenæum.*

" Henry Westgate, the hero, is a study of no slight psychological interest. . . . It is the development of this character for good and for evil, through the diverse influence of friends and circumstances . . . . that Miss George has portrayed with singular vigour and skilful analysis. . . . It is impossible to read this story without wonderment at the maturity and self-restraint of its style, and at the rare beauty and pathos, mingled with strength, which mark every page."—*Literary World.*

GEORGE REDWAY, YORK STREET, COVENT GARDEN.

In demy 8vo., with Illustrative Plates.   Price 1s.

Chirognomancy;

Or, Indications of Temperament and Aptitudes Manifested by the Form and Texture of the Thumb and Fingers.

BY

ROSA BAUGHAN.

" Miss Baughan has already established her fame as a writer upon occult subjects, and what she has to say is so very clear and so easily verified that it comes with the weight of authority."—*Lady's Pictorial.*

GEORGE REDWAY, YORK STREET, COVENT GARDEN.

REDWAY'S SHILLING SERIES, VOL. III.

An édition de luxe, in demy 18mo.

Tobacco Talk and Smokers' Gossip.

An Amusing Miscellany of Fact and Anecdote relating to
" The Great Plant " in all its Forms and Uses, including
a Selection from Nicotian Literature.

" One of the best books of gossip we have met for some time. . . . It is literally crammed full from beginning to end of its 148 pages with well-selected anecdotes, poems, and excerpts from tobacco literature and history."—*Graphic.*

" The smoker should be grateful to the compilers of this pretty little volume. . . . No smoker should be without it, and anti-tobacconists have only to turn over its leaves to be converted."—*Pall Mall Gazette.*

" Something to please smokers ; and non-smokers may be interested in tracing the effect of tobacco—the fatal, fragrant herb—on our literature."— *Literary World.*

GEORGE REDWAY, YORK STREET, COVENT GARDEN.

In crown 8vo., parchment. Price 3s. 6d.

The Anatomy of Tobacco;

Or, Smoking Methodised, Divided, and Considered after a New Fashion.

BY

LEOLINUS SILURIENSIS.

" A very clever and amusing parody of the metaphysical treatises once in fashion. Every smoker will be pleased with this volume."—*Notes and Queries.*

" We have here a most excellent piece of fooling, evidently from a University pen. . . . contains some very clever burlesques of classical modes of writing, and a delicious parody of scholastic logic."—*Literary World.*

" A delightful mock essay on the exoteric philosophy of the pipe and the pipe bowl . . . . reminding one alternately of 'Melancholy' Burton and Herr Teufelsdröch, and implying vast reading and out-of-the-way culture on the part of the author."— *Bookseller.*

GEORGE REDWAY, YORK STREET, COVENT GARDEN.

An edition de luxe, in demy 18mo. Price 1s.

Confessions of an English Hachish Eater.

"There is a sort of bizarre attraction in this fantastic little book, with its weird, unhealthy imaginations."— *Whitehall Review.*

"Imagination or some other faculty plays marvellous freaks in this little book." — *Lloyd's Weekly.*

"A charmingly written and not less charmingly printed little volume. The anonymous author describes his experiences in language which for picturesqueness is worthy to rank with De Quincey's celebrated sketch of the English Opium Eater."—*Lincolnshire Chronicle.*

"A weird little book. . . . The author seems to have been delighted with his dreams, and . . . . carefully explains how hachish may be made from the resin of the common hemp plant."--*Daily Chronicle.*

"To be added to the literature of what is, after all, a very undesirable subject. Weak minds may generate a morbid curiosity if stimulated in this direction."—*Bradford Observer.*

"The stories told by our author have a decidedly Oriental flavour, and we would not be surprised if some foolish individuals did endeavour to procure some of the drug, with a view to experience the sensation described by the writer of this clever brochure."—*Edinburgh Courant.*

GEORGE REDWAY, YORK STREET, COVENT GARDEN.

Monthly, One Shilling.

Walford's Antiquarian :

A Magazine and Bibliographical Review.

EDITED BY

EDWARD WALFORD, M.A.

** *Volumes I. to VII., Now Ready, price 8s. 6d.*

GEORGE REDWAY, YORK STREET, COVENT GARDEN.

THE ONLY PUBLISHED BIOGRAPHY OF JOHN LEECH.

An édition de luxe in demy 18mo.   *Price 1s.*

John Leech,

ARTIST AND HUMOURIST.

A BIOGRAPHICAL SKETCH.

BY

FRED. G. KITTON.

New Edition, revised.

" In the absence of a fuller biography we cordially welcome Mr. Kitton's interesting little sketch."—*Notes and Queries.*

" The multitudinous admirers of the famous artist will find this touching monograph well worth careful reading and preservation."—*Daily Chronicle.*

" The very model of what such a memoir should be."—*Graphic.*

GEORGE REDWAY, YORK STREET, COVENT GARDEN.

Third Edition, newly revised, in demy 8vo., with Illustrative Plates.
Price 1s.

The Handbook of Palmistry,

Including an Account of the Doctrines of the Kabbala.

BY

R. BAUGHAN,

AUTHOR OF "INDICATIONS OF CHARACTER IN HANDWRITING."

" It possesses a certain literary interest, for Miss Baughan shows the connection between palmistry and the doctrines of the Kabbala."—*Graphic.*

" Miss Rosa Baughan, for many years known as one of the most expert proficients in this branch of science, has as much claim to consideration as any writer on the subject."—*Sussex Daily News.*

" People who wish to believe in palmistry, or the science of reading character from the marks of the hand," says the *Daily News,* in an article devoted to the discussion of this topic, "will be interested in a handbook of the subject by Miss Baughan, published by Mr. Redway."

GEORGE REDWAY, YORK STREET, COVENT GARDEN.

EBENEZER JONES'S POEMS.

In post 8vo., cloth, old style. Price 5s.

Studies of Sensation and Event.

Poems by EBENEZER JONES.

Edited, Prefaced, and Annotated by RICHARD HERNE SHEPHERD.

With Memorial Notices of the Author by SUMNER JONES and W. J. LINTON.

A new Edition. With Photographic Portrait of the Poet.

"This remarkable poet affords nearly the most striking instance of neglected genius in our modern school of poetry. His poems are full of vivid disorderly power."—D. G. ROSSETTI.

GEORGE REDWAY, YORK STREET, COVENT GARDEN.

In demy 8vo., elegantly printed on Dutch hand-made paper, and bound in parchment-paper cover. Price 1s.

The Scope and Charm of Antiquarian Study.

BY

JOHN BATTY, F.R.Hist.S.,

MEMBER OF THE YORKSHIRE ARCHÆOLOGICAL AND TOPOGRAPICAL ASSOCIATION.

"It forms a useful and entertaining guide to a beginner in historical researches."—*Notes and Queries.*

"The author has laid it before the public in a most inviting, intelligent, and intelligible form, and offers every incentive to the study in every department, including Ancient Records, Manorial Court-Rolls, Heraldry, Painted Glass, Mural Paintings, Pottery, Church Bells, Numismatics, Folk-Lore, etc., to each of which the attention of the student is directed. The pamphlet is printed on a beautiful modern antique paper, appropriate to the subject of the work."—*Brighton Examiner.*

"Mr. Batty, who is one of those folks Mr. Dobson styles 'gleaners after time,' has clearly and concisely summed up, in the space of a few pages, all the various objects which may legitimately be considered to come within the scope of antiquarian study."—*Academy.*

GEORGE REDWAY, YORK STREET, COVENT GARDEN.

A few large-paper copies, with India proof portrait, in imperial 8vo., parchment. Price 7s. 6d.

An Essay on the Genius of George Cruikshank.

BY

"THETA" (WILLIAM MAKEPEACE THACKERAY).

With all the Original Woodcut Illustrations, a New Portrait of CRUIKSHANK, etched by PAILTHORPE, and a Prefatory Note on THACKERAY AS AN ART CRITIC, by W. E. CHURCH, Secretary of the Urban Club.

" Thackeray's essay 'On the Genius of George Cruikshank,' reprinted from the *Westminster Review*, is a piece of work well calculated to drive a critic of these days to despair. How inimitable is its touch! At once familiar and elegant, serious and humorous, enthusiastically appreciative, and yet just and clear-sighted ; but, above all, what the French call *personnel*. It is not the impersonnel reviewer who is going through his paces . . . it is Thackeray talking to us as few can talk—talking with apparent carelessness, even ramblingly, but never losing the thread of his discourse or saying a word too much, nor ever missing a point which may help to elucidate his subject or enhance the charm of his essay. . . . Mr. W. E. Church's prefatory note on 'Thackeray as an Art Critic' is interesting and carefully compiled."—*Westminster Review*, Jan. 15th.

"As the original copy of the *Westminster* is now excessively rare, this reissue will, no doubt, be welcomed by collectors."—*Birmingham Daily Mail.*

"Not only on account of the author, but of the object, we must welcome most cordially this production. Every bookman knows Thackeray, and will be glad to have this production of his which deals with art criticism—a subject so peculiarly Thackeray's own."—*The Antiquary.*

"It was a pleasant and not untimely act to reprint this well-known delightful essay. . . . the artist could have found no other commentator so sympathetic and discriminating. . . . The new portrait of Cruikshank by F. W. Pailthorpe is a clear, firm etching."—*The Artist.*

GEORGE REDWAY, YORK STREET, COVENT GARDEN.

In crown 8vo., cloth. Price 7s. 6d.

Theosophy, Religion, and Occult Science.

BY

HENRY S. OLCOTT,

PRESIDENT OF THE THEOSOPHICAL SOCIETY.

WITH GLOSSARY OF EASTERN WORDS.

———

"This book, to which we can only allot an amount of space quite incommensurate with its intrinsic interest, is one that will appeal to the prepared student rather than to the general reader. To anyone who has previously made the acquaintance of such as Mr. Sinnett's 'Occult World,' and 'Esoteric Buddhism,' or has in other ways familiarised himself with the doctrines of the so-called Theosophical Society or Brotherhood, these lectures of Colonel Olcott's will be rich in interest and suggestiveness. The American officer is a person of undoubted social position and unblemished personal reputation, and his main object is not to secure belief in the reality of any 'phenomena,' not to win a barren reputation for himself as a thaumaturgist or wonder-worker, but to win acceptance for one of the oldest philosophies of nature and human life—a philosophy to which of late years the thinkers of the West have been turning with noteworthy curiosity and interest. Of course, should the genuineness of the phenomena in question be satisfactorily established, there would undoubtedly be proof that the Eastern sages to whom Colonel Olcott bears witness do possess a knowledge of the laws of the physical universe far wider and more intimate than that which has been laboriously acquired by the inductive science of the West; but the theosophy expounded in this volume is at once a theology, a metaphysic, and a sociology, in which mere marvels, as such, occupy a quite subordinate and unimportant position. We cannot now discuss its claims, and we will [not pronounce any opinion upon them; we will only say that Colonel Olcott's volume deserves and will repay the study of all readers for whom the bye-ways of speculation have an irresistible charm." —*Manchester Examiner.*

———

GEORGE REDWAY, YORK STREET COVENT GARDEN.

Monthly, 2s.; Yearly Subscription, **20s.**

The Theosophist:

A Magazine of Oriental Philosophy, Art, Literature and Occultism.

CONDUCTED BY

H. P. BLAVATSKY.

Vols. I. to VI. Now Ready.

"Theosophy has suddenly risen to importance. . . . The movement implied by the term Theosophy is one that cannot be adequately explained in a few words . . . those interested in the movement, which is not to be confounded with spiritualism, will find means of gratifying their curiosity by procuring the back numbers of *The Theosophist* and a very remarkable book call 'Isis Unveiled,' by Madame Blavatsky."—*Literary World.*

GEORGE REDWAY, YORK STREET, COVENT GARDEN.

NEW WORK BY JOHN H. INGRAM.

The Raven.

BY

EDGAR ALLAN POE.

With Historical and Literary Commentary.   By JOHN H. INGRAM.

Crown 8vo., parchment, gilt top, uncut, price 6s.

"This is an interesting monograph on Poe's famous poem. First comes the poet's own account of the genesis of the poem, with a criticism, in which Mr. Ingram declines, very properly, we think, to accept the history as entirely genuine. Much curious information is collected in this essay. Then follows the poem itself, with the various readings, and then its after-history; and after these 'Isadore,' by Albert Pike, a composition which undoubtedly suggested the idea of 'The Raven' to its author. Several translations are given, two in French, one in prose, the other in rhymed verse; besides extracts from others, two in German and one in Latin. But perhaps the most interesting chapter in the book is that on the 'Fabrications.'"—*The Spectator.*

"There is no more reliable authority on the subject of Edgar Allan Poe than Mr. John H. Ingram . . . the volume is well printed and tastefully bound in spotless vellum, and will prove to be a work of the greatest interest to all students of English and American literature."—*The Publishers' Circular.*

GEORGE REDWAY, YORK STREET, COVENT GARDEN.

NEW REALISTIC NOVEL.

620 *pages, handsomely bound.* Price 6s.

Leicester :

AN AUTOBIOGRAPHY.

BY

FRANCIS W. L. ADAMS.

"Even M. Zola and Mr. George Moore would find it hard to beat Mr Adams's description of Rosy's death. The grimly minute narrative of Leicester's schoolboy troubles and of his attempt to get a living when he is discarded by his guardian is, too, of such a character as to make one regret that Mr. Adams had not put to better use his undoubted, though undisciplined, powers."—*The Academy.*

"There is unquestionable power in 'Leicester.'"—*The Athenæum.*

GEORGE REDWAY, YORK STREET, COVENT GARDEN.

NEW BOOK BY MISS BAUGHAN.

The Handbook of Physiognomy.

BY

ROSA BAUGHAN

Demy 8vo., wrapper, Price 1s.

CONTENTS.—Chapter 1. "The Face is the Mirror of the Soul." II. The Forehead and Eyebrows. III. The Eyes and Eyelashes. IV. The Nose. V. The Mouth, Teeth, Jaw, and Chin. VI. The Hair and the Ears. VII. The Complexion. VIII. Congenial Faces. IX. The Signatures of the Planets on the Face. X. Pathognomy.

GEORGE REDWAY, YORK STREET, COVENT GARDEN.

Small 4to., with Illustrations, bound in vegetable parchment.
Price 10s. 6d.

THE

Virgin of the World:

BY HERMES MERCURIUS TRISMEGISTUS.

A Treatise on INITIATIONS, or ASCLEPIOS ; the DEFI-
NITIONS of ASCLEPIOS ; FRAGMENTS of the
WRITINGS of HERMES.

TRANSLATED AND EDITED BY THE AUTHORS OF "THE PERFECT
WAY."

With an Introduction to "The Virgin of the World" by A. K.,
and an Essay on "The Hermetic Books" by E. M.

———

"It will be a most interesting study for every occultist to compare the
doctrines of the ancient Hermetic philosophy with the teaching of the
Vedantic and Buddhist systems of religious thought. The famous books of
Hermes seem to occupy, with reference to the Egyptian religion, the same
position which the Upanishads occupy in Aryan religious literature."—
The Theosophist, November, 1885.

———

GEORGE REDWAY, YORK STREET, COVENT GARDEN.

In preparation.

NEW TRANSLATION OF "THE HEPTAMERON."

THE "JOHN PAYNE" EDITION.

The Heptameron ;

OR,

Tales and Novels of Margaret, Queen of Navarre.

Now first done completely into English prose and verse, from the original French, by ARTHUR MACHEN.

With an Introduction by JOHN PAYNE, Translator of "The Poems of Master Francis Villon, of Paris," "The Book of the Thousand Nights and One Night," etc.

GEORGE REDWAY, YORK STREET, COVENT GARDEN.

One vol., crown 8vo., 400 pages. Price 6s.

A Regular Pickle :

How He Sowed his Wild Oats.

BY

HENRY W. NESFIELD.

"Mr. Nesfield's name as an author is established on such a pleasantly sound foundation that it is a recognised fact that, in taking up a book written by him, the reader is in for a delightful half-hour, during which his risible and humorous faculties will be pleasantly stimulated. The history of young Archibald Highton Tregauntly, whose fortunes we follow from the cradle to when experience is just beginning to teach him a few wholesome lessons, is as smart and brisk as it is possible to be."—*Whitehall Review.*

"It will be matter for regret if the brisk and lively style of Mr. Nesfield, who at times reminds us of Lever, should blind people to the downright wickedness of such a perverted career as is here described."—*Daily Chronicle.*

GEORGE REDWAY, YORK STREET, COVENT GARDEN.

Fourth Edition.   With Engraved Frontispiece.   In crown 8vo., 5s.

Cosmo de' Medici:

An Historical Tragedy.   And other Poems.

BY

RICHARD HENGIST HORNE,

Author of " Orion."

" This tragedy is the work of a poet and not of a playwright. Many of the scenes abound in vigour and tragic intensity.   If the structure of the drama challenges comparison with the masterpieces of the Elizabethan stage, it is at least not unworthy of the models which have inspired it."—*Times.*

GEORGE REDWAY, YORK STREET, COVENT GARDEN.

Fcap. 8vo., parchment.

Tamerlane and other Poems.

BY

EDGAR ALLAN POE.

First published at Boston in 1827, and now first republished from a unique copy of the original edition, with a preface by RICHARD HERNE SHEPHERD.

Mr. Swinburne has generously praised "so beautiful and valuable a little volume, full of interest for the admirers of Poe's singular and exquisite genius."

GEORGE REDWAY, YORK STREET, COVENT GARDEN.

Just ready, in demy 8vo., choicely printed, and bound in Japanese parchment. Price 7s. 6d.

Primitive Symbolism

As Illustrated in Phallic Worship; or, The Reproductive Principle.

BY

The late HODDER M. WESTROPP.

With an Introduction by GENERAL FORLONG, Author of "Rivers of Life."

"This work is a *multum in parvo* of the growth and spread of Phallicism, as we commonly call the worship of nature or fertilizing powers. I felt, when solicited to enlarge and illustrate it on the sudden death of the lamented author, that it would be desecration to touch so complete a compendium by one of the most competent and soundest thinkers who have written on this world-wide faith. None knew better or saw more clearly than Mr. Westropp that in this oldest symbolism and worship lay the foundations of all the goodly systems we call religions."—J. G. R. FORLONG.

GEORGE REDWAY, YORK STREET, COVENT GARDEN.

In large crown 8vo. Price 3s. 6d.

Sithron, the Star Stricken.

Translated (*Ala bereket Allah*) from an ancient Arabic Manuscript.

BY

SALEM BEN UZÄIR, of Bassora.

"This very remarkable book, 'Sithron'... is a bold, pungent, audacious satire upon the ancient religious belief of the Jews. ... No one can read the book without homage to the force, the tenderness, and the never-failing skill of its writer."—*St. James's Gazette.*

GEORGE REDWAY, YORK STREET, COVENT GARDEN.

Post free, price 3d.

The Literature of Occultism and Archæology.

Being a Catalogue of Books ON SALE relating to

Ancient Worships.
Astrology.
Alchemy.
Animal Magnetism.
Anthropology.
Arabic.
Assassins.
Antiquities.
Ancient History.
Behmen and the Mystics.
Buddhism.
Clairvoyance.
Cabeiri.
China.
Coins.
Druids.
Dreams and Visions.
Divination.
Divining Rod.
Demonology.
Ethnology.
Egypt.
Fascination.
Flagellants.
Freemasonry.
Folk-Lore.
Gnostics.
Gems.
Ghosts.
Hindus.
Hieroglyphics and Secret Writing.
Herbals.
Hermetic.
India and the Hindus.
Kabbala.
Koran.
Miracles.
Mirabilaries.

Magic and Magicians.
Mysteries.
Mithraic Worship
Mesmerism.
Mythology.
Metaphysics.
Mysticism.
Neo-platonism.
Orientalia.
Obelisks.
Oracles.
Occult Sciences.
Phallic Worship.
Philology.
Persian.
Parsees.
Philosophy.
Physiognomy.
Palmistry and Handwriting.
Phrenology.
Psychoneurology.
Psychometry.
Prophets.
Rosicrucians.
Round Towers.
Rabbinical.
Spiritualism.
Skeptics, Jesuits, Christians and Quakers.
Sibylls.
Symbolism.
Serpent Worship.
Secret Societies.
Somnambulism.
Travels.
Tombs.
Theosophical.
Theology and Criticism.
Witchcraft.

GEORGE REDWAY, YORK STREET, COVENT GARDEN.

In preparation.

The Praise of Ale ;

OR,

Songs, Ballads, Epigrams, and Anecdotes relating to

Beer, Malt, and Hops.

Collected and arranged by

W. MARCHANT.

Send for Prospectus.

GEORGE REDWAY, YORK STREET, COVENT GARDEN.

In preparation.

Park's History and Topography of Hampstead.

Revised and brought down to the Present Time.

BY

EDWARD WALFORD, M.A.,

Editor of " Walford's Antiquarian."

Send for Prospectus.

GEORGE REDWAY, YORK STREET, COVENT GARDEN.

REDWAYS SHILLING SERIES,

Nearly ready, Vol. IV.

Wellerisms.

EDITED BY

CHARLES KENT.

A collection of all the " good things " for which the Wellers, *père et fils*, are famous—a posy culled from the pages of *Pickwick* and *Master Humphrey's Clock*.

GEORGE REDWAY, YORK STREET, COVENT GARDEN.

Nearly ready.

The Curate's Wife.

A NOVEL.

BY

Mrs. J. E. PANTON,

Author of "Sketches in Black and White."

GEORGE REDWAY, YORK STREET, COVENT GARDEN.

Nearly ready.

The History of the Forty Vezirs;

OR,

The Story of the Forty Morns and Eves,

Written in Turkish by SHEYKH-ZADA, and now done into English by E. J. W. GIBB, M.R.A.S.

GEORGE REDWAY, YORK STREET, COVENT GARDEN.

In preparation.

Sea Songs and River Rhymes.

A SELECTION OF ENGLISH VERSE, FROM CHAUCER TO SWINBURNE.

EDITED BY

Mrs. DAVENPORT ADAMS.

With Etchings by Mackaness.

This is a Collection of Poems and Passages by English Writers on the subject of the Sea and Rivers, and covers the whole of the ground between Spenser and Tennyson. It includes numerous copyright Poems, for the reproduction of which the author and publishers have given their permission.

GEORGE REDWAY, YORK STREET, COVENT GARDEN.

Nearly ready.

Essays in the Study of Folk-Songs.

BY

THE COUNTESS EVELYN MARTINENGO-CESARESCO.

CONTENTS:

INTRODUCTION.
THE INSPIRATION OF DEATH IN FOLK-POETRY.
NATURE IN FOLK-SONGS.
ARMENIAN FOLK-SONGS.
VENETIAN FOLK-SONGS.
SICILIAN FOLK-SONGS.
GREEK SONGS OF CALABRIA.
FOLK-SONGS OF PROVENCE.
THE WHITE PATERNOSTER.
THE DIFFUSION OF BALLADS.
SONGS FOR THE RITE OF MAY.
THE IDEA OF FATE IN SOUTHERN TRADITIONS.
FOLK-LULLABIES.
FOLK-DIRGES.

GEORGE REDWAY, YORK STREET, COVENT GARDEN.

*Shortly will be published in 8vo. handsomely printed on antique
paper, and tastefully bound. Price 1s. to Subscribers.*

Pope Joan

(*THE FEMALE POPE*).

A Historical Study.   Translated from the Greek of Emmanuel
Rhoïdis, with Preface by

CHARLES HASTINGS COLLETTE.

"The subject of POPE JOAN has not yet lost the interest which belongs to it,
as a fact in the province of historical criticism."—*Dr. Döllinger.*

THE PLAYS OF GEORGE COLMAN THE YOUNGER.

The Comedies and Farces

OF

GEORGE COLMAN THE YOUNGER.

Now first collected and carefully reprinted from the Original Editions,
with Annotations and Critical and Bibliographical Preface,

BY

RICHARD HERNE SHEPHERD.

In Two Volumes.

Some of these plays have become very scarce ; and of those which have kept
the stage, the text has been more or less corrupted.

NEWLY-DISCOVERED POEM BY CHARLES LAMB.

Beauty and the Beast.

A Story in Verse for Children by CHARLES LAMB.   Now first
reprinted from the Unique Original, with Preface and Notes

BY

RICHARD HERNE SHEPHERD.

Only 100 Copies printed.

GEORGE REDWAY, YORK STREET, COVENT GARDEN.

www.ingramcontent.com/pod-product-compliance
Lightning Source LLC
Chambersburg PA
CBHW020028030726
47499CB00007B/2316